Dead Ball Foul

Kayla McGrady

SILVER DAGGER
M Y S T E R I E S

Hardcover ISBN 1-57072-117-3
Trade Paper ISBN 1-57072-133-5
Copyright © 2000 by Kayla McGrady
Printed in the United States of America
All Rights Reserved

1 2 3 4 5 6 7 8 9 0

For Ed,

who helped me find my dream:
without you, none of this would be possible.

ACKNOWLEDGMENTS

I would like to give my very sincere thanks to David Hunter and to Investigator J. P. Bledsoe of the Scott County (Virginia) Police Department for explaining quite a few points about police procedure. I would also like to thank Sam McGrady (Dad) for answering about a million and one questions concerning football, Becky McGrady (Mom) for coming up with a great title, and Kristin Norris (Big Sister) who relayed the final edit back to the publisher while I was away from home with no Internet access—I love you guys!!! Melissa Burgess, Ed Price, and Sherry Lewis deserve a big pat on the back for putting in so much work to help me make *Dead Ball Foul* the best book it could be. I would really like to give heartfelt thanks to my family and friends who have been there for me and given me support through everything and to Liz Squire, my mentor, and the rest of my Silver Dagger family who have offered encouragement and helped me through the confusing process of publishing my first book. I cannot thank Joe McMurray and Daniel Hall enough for their unending interest and support from start to finish— their enthusiasm has made more of a difference than they ever realized. Gate City High School and its varsity football team deserve acknowledgment for providing me with inspiration and helping me to grow a great love for high school football (Virginia AA Division 3 State Champions, 1997). And last, but certainly not least, I would like to thank God, who gave me every single word written on the pages that follow.

CHAPTER ONE

BEEEP—BEEEP—BEEEP.

"Hmm?" I muttered as I rolled over. I blindly reached over and smacked at the squealing alarm clock. On the third swing, I finally hit the right button.

"I'm awake, I'm awake," I mumbled as I opened my eyes and squinted against the unwelcome light. Another day. I threw my legs over the side of my bed and sat up. I guess no teenager ever really gets used to waking up in the morning, and I was no exception. I stood up and stumbled through the automatic motions of getting ready for school.

It was late September, and I was finishing up my fourth week in the eleventh grade at W. H. Carrier High. Get this—our school was named for W. H. Carrier, the American inventor of the air conditioner. Sure, it gets hot around here in the summer and we all appreciate our air conditioners, but really! Oh well, I guess it's better than being named after the father of American football. They say that our school was almost named Walter Camp High, but that name got vetoed by some of the committee members. They settled for naming our football stadium Walter Camp Field, instead. I think I'd rather go to Carrier High than Camp High, anyway. This town was obsessed enough with football as it was.

I brushed through my black hair a few times, parted it, and threw the beaten-up, half-dead brush into my backpack. I paused for a moment to inspect myself in the mirror. To tell the truth, there wasn't really anything remarkable about my appearance. I was one of those unfortunate girls stuck in the middle of everything. I wasn't fat, but I wasn't skinny. I wasn't tall, but I wasn't short. I never tanned much, but I didn't have beautiful ivory skin, either. I definitely wasn't ugly, but I wasn't strikingly gorgeous. I was, in fact, just plain old Tricia Lakely.

To make matters worse, I was at that awkward age when everything seemed at least twice as complicated as it really was.

I never seemed to get a moment's rest. Whenever I wasn't paying attention, my emotions would make me do or think something completely irrational. My brain and my heart were engaged in constant war. My heart professed what I felt—my brain argued what I should be feeling. To say the least, times were interesting.

Hoisting my backpack onto my shoulder, I turned from the mirror, deciding my appearance would do. I trotted down the steps, went into the kitchen to give Mom a kiss, and headed outside. Tossing my backpack into the passenger side of my truck, I climbed in. I backed out of my driveway and pulled onto Horizon Drive.

Some say teenagers take their vehicles for granted, but I certainly didn't. I had been saving money since I was about five for this truck, a little blue Toyota. I appreciated my truck very, very much. I suppose you could say it meant freedom, in a different sense of the word. It wasn't as if I could take off and go anywhere anytime I wanted, but instead of asking, "Mom, can you take me?" I just asked, "Mom, can I go?" It simplified things a great deal.

Don't get me wrong—Mom always had to know where I was, how late I'd be out, and even then she didn't always say yes. But I think it was a load off her shoulders when she stopped having to juggle both of our schedules.

I chuckled as I passed the familiar sign that read JUDSONVILLE CORPORATE LIMITS. True, some of the residents considered the fact that our town was named after the inventor of the zipper a bit embarrassing, but most of us were pretty philosophical about it. It's just a name, I suppose—better than some I've heard.

There's a great deal of mystery concerning how the town got its name in the first place. No one knows what happened when the founders met in 1899, but when the meeting was finally over, the proposal to name the town "Judsonville" had been signed by everyone there—the minutes read that it had been a unanimous vote. Some say the founders were drugged by a prankster. Some say the ghost of Thomas Jefferson appeared and told them to do it. The truth is, no one knows. The name has been challenged only once since then—the protest ended in an old-fashioned free-for-all in the Carrier High parking lot where the status quo faction won out.

There it was: Carrier High. Maybe our school wasn't all that impressive, but that wasn't important to most of its students.

It was still home. There was no brand new school sign or huge three-floor school building. In fact, our high school had only two halls—Long Hall and Short Hall—and only Short Hall had an upstairs.

The old brick high school was in pretty good shape—considering the fact that it was about as old as Judsonville—even though most of the lockers looked like they were about to fall off the wall. Nevertheless, there was a noticeable contrast between the high school and the middle school, added on only ten years ago to make a complex.

The middle school had three floors, a bigger gym with a better floor, and even desks that didn't fall apart when people sat in them. Everything in the middle school was still shiny (except for the bathroom stalls which had been scrubbed to remove graffiti about a hundred times too many). Still, once I had moved up into the high school in the tenth grade, the high school grew on me in a way I could never explain. I guess it just felt more homey and a tad bit friendlier and more informal.

The kids in the next county at Stonewall Jackson High in Bucknersville, a nearby town, taunted us about how tiny our school was. In truth, it wasn't all that small (there were two much smaller high schools in another neighboring county), but Jackson High was about twice the size of Carrier High. They would tease us about the names of both our town and school.

Most of the time we were nice enough not to point out that Bucknersville and Jackson High weren't really great names either. After all, U. S. Grant kicked Simon Bolivar Buckner's butt at Fort Henry, and Stonewall Jackson was mistakenly shot by his own men at Chancellorsville. How great is that? But when a member of our student body would occasionally respond to the bad jokes with one of these objections, the Jackson kids would proudly point out that at least their town and school were named after generals. We were stuck with inventors. Our only consolation was the fact that we always beat Jackson at football.

I pulled into the familiar parking space that I had claimed at the beginning of the year. We didn't actually have assigned parking spaces, but everybody always parked in the same place anyway, so it didn't matter. I parked there mostly for convenience, but another very big reason was the little gray Chevy parked right next to my Toyota. Luke's truck.

Luke had begun working his way into my heart sometime at the end of last year. I knew that guys were nothing but trouble, but my heart wasn't listening. I mean, maybe he was nice, but he was nothing like my friends' description of the "perfect man." He didn't drive an awesome car, he wasn't rich, he wasn't incredibly gorgeous, and he wasn't some popular jock. In fact, rumor had it that he was fast enough to be a track star, but he never showed much interest in athletics. All I could figure out was that maybe, unlike my friends, my idea of *perfect* was an average, ordinary guy—like Luke, for example.

I slung my backpack over my shoulder, dropped my keys into my pocket, and walked through the big double doors into Carrier High. I made my way through the halls lined with students seated on the floor in front of the lockers. The halls were really the only place to hang out before the first bell, the signal for the teachers to start unlocking their doors. Most of these early birds were sophomores, but a few of my fellow juniors were scattered into the mix as well. There were almost no seniors, though. They seemed to have a tendency to arrive somewhat later—like three or four minutes before the tardy bell rang.

Aaron Tyler, an old friend, sat near the end of the hall with his girlfriend, Jackie Carrico. I flinched as I passed them. Aaron was a senior (not to mention a football player) whom I had known quite well the year before when we had had a class together. I had actually daydreamed of becoming more than friends. Unfortunately, I hadn't spoken to him in almost a year now, even though all dreams of romance were gone and all I wanted was a renewed friendship. Maybe, if I was lucky, I'd work my courage up a day or two before graduation.

I dumped my books into my locker, a bit disgusted with myself for being such a wuss. I pulled out what I needed for first block and headed down the hall. I caught sight of my friend Melissa Hall waiting for me. I smiled and sat down next to her. "Hey," I greeted.

She gave me a sleepy smile. Yawning, she brushed a lock of her curly brown hair behind her ear. "I think I'll sleep through biology."

"Oh well," I replied. "You can wake up in second."

Our school ran on block scheduling, which meant that each day was composed of four classes, each ninety minutes long. Our classes changed halfway through the year, and we had four different classes second semester. Second block this semester Melissa and I had chorus together. Who could sleep through an hour and a half of chorus? "Look at it this way, sweetie," I said. "At least *you* can sleep through biology. Not possible for me in history. Not with Mr. Burton's booming voice."

"Isn't it a bit early to be discussing Burton's lectures? Let's not cross that bridge until we absolutely have to." I looked up to see another friend, Rachael Blair.

She was dressed in the usual jeans/tennis shoes with her blonde hair tied back in its customary ponytail. The only thing about Rachael's appearance that ever really changed was her shirt. She had a whole closet full of shirts of all kinds—but all matched jeans and sneakers. I had yet to see my skinny, blonde friend in a skirt. She'd be melting male hearts for sure, but she absolutely refused. She said that dresses and skirts were (A) sexist and (B) exceedingly uncomfortable.

Rachael understood about Mr. Burton all too well. She had U.S. History with me first block. Mr. Burton could probably wake the dead through a dozen panes of soundproof glass if he really tried.

Rachael sat down beside Melissa. "You look tired," Rachael commented. Then she smiled. "Well, here's something to wake you up. Have you seen the new guy on Horizon Drive?"

Melissa perked up immediately. "The one who moved into that log house that the Fergusons were trying forever to sell?"

Rachael's green eyes twinkled. "Yeah. The one who lives right across the road from Tricia."

"My dad told us about him," Melissa said. "I saw him on my way out to the store yesterday." Melissa's dad was a cop—he missed very little of what was going on in Judsonville. Of course, a big moving van parked in front of a previously empty house is pretty much a dead giveaway. Melissa gave me an envious look. "It's not fair!"

"Why?" I asked.

"Because . . . ," she began, pausing to find the perfect words to explain it to me.

Rachael settled for simplicity. "Because he is *fine*, Tricia."

Melissa sighed. "You know, Rachael," she said with a dreamy smile, "we should invite ourselves over to Tricia's house and, out of innocent neighborliness of course, we should give Mr. New Guy the proper welcome."

"Oh, come on, you guys. He's got to be almost thirty."

"So?" Melissa shot back.

"That's more than ten years older than you!" I exclaimed. "It would be like going out with . . . with Bobby Joe Fink!"

Melissa and Rachael exchanged slightly sick looks. "I definitely wouldn't put it in that light," Rachael protested.

Bobby Joe Fink was our janitor. He may have been only twenty-eight, but he looked forty. The poor guy had one of those stiff faces that hardly ever smiled—maybe because the world had poured too much vinegar in his Cheerios. He seemed like a pretty cynical person. I couldn't really blame him—after I graduated I certainly wouldn't want to be stuck back in the same old high school sweeping nasty floors and scrubbing toilets. Bobby Joe seemed to be a whole generation away from us, even though there was little more than a decade's difference.

Melissa gave in. "Okay, scratch that idea."

Rachael gracefully stood up (just about everything Rachael did was graceful) as the bell rang to warn us we had five minutes to get to class. I climbed to my feet, offered the sleepy Melissa a hand, and pulled her up.

"We can still say he's cute, though," Rachael said over her shoulder with a grin, her blonde ponytail swishing mischievously as she walked away.

Algebra was evil—specifically Algebra II, my last class. Math always put me in the dumps. I climbed into my truck after school but didn't bother to start it. I just sat there and stared into space.

Directly across the street, a huge sign hung on the back of the stadium. All around the edges, dates were etched in blue: 1971, 1975, 1979. . . . These were years that Carrier High held the state title in football. The dates were so old, older than I was. . . . All but one. This one stood boldly in thick blue numerals. Last year's date. The first time we had been state champs in two decades.

Painted in the center of these moments of victory was the rearing image of the Carrier High Mustang, our "sacred" mascot. I thought of our eccentric founders and smiled. At least they had given our school a mascot unrelated to its name. What if they had picked the "Carrier Eagles" or the "Carrier Storks" or something like that? We would never have been able to hold our heads up in front of the kids from Jackson.

I turned the key, and my truck sputtered to life. As I started down the road I flipped on the radio. I was hoping for a cheerful song, but I got a mournful tune about lost love. "Oh, why doesn't she love me, I'm losing my mind, lah-de-dah," or something to that effect. I disgustedly changed the station and caught the chords of a song I liked—naturally it was the ending.

I waited impatiently for another upbeat song, but instead the DJ was talking about some drug bust gone bad up in Roanoke. The cops had nabbed the buyer and the drugs, but the pusher had gotten away with the money. Roanoke seemed like a whole world away. Nothing exciting ever happened here.

I drove past old Roscoe Thompson's place. Judsonville wasn't necessarily your average, ordinary town, but the strangest part about it (besides the abnormal obsession with football) was old Roscoe.

He ran a used car lot, but everyone suspected that he had a darker side. He hardly ever seemed to sell one of his junky cars, yet he got along fine himself. I'd heard people speculate that he was a loan shark. Of course, a relatively quiet little place like Judsonville was kind of a strange place for a loan shark to set up shop, but I supposed anything was possible.

I was tired of hearing about drug busts in Roanoke and thinking about Roscoe Thompson, so I turned the station again and was finally greeted by a tune that sure beat all of that other depressing stuff. I turned up the radio, rolled down my window, and let the breeze and the song guide me home.

I was ready to scream at my algebra book—again! I threw my pencil onto the textbook and sat there glaring at it. I flinched as the phone rang. Giving my book one more spiteful look, I stuck my tongue out at it as I got up and headed for the phone. "Hello?" I said, trying not to sound as irritated as I felt.

"Hello, Tricia," replied a crackled old voice.

I smiled. "Hello, Grandma Harriet!"

Grandma Harriet lived in Stockton, about half an hour away. Grandma was old and frail, and I had been spending every summer with her since I was eleven to help her out. I loved my grandmother dearly and was glad to hear from her. "How are you?"

"Fine, fine, but a bit lonely. Why don't you come and visit

your old granny next weekend?"

"You have Paul right next door," I pointed out.

"Paul misses you, too."

I smiled again. "Well I miss Paul. And you, too."

Paul was Grandma Harriet's next-door neighbor. He was a nice young man with beautiful roses growing in his front yard and a good sense of humor. Grandma and I liked him, but then everybody probably did. Paul had thrown me a surprise party for my sixteenth birthday just before I left. He was one of the nicest people I'd ever met, almost like the big brother I never had.

"Oh dear," she mumbled. "I just remembered. Next week's Homecoming, isn't it?"

"So what? I can still come. I'll stop by after school and drop my things off. Then I'll head back for the game, and you and I can have all day Saturday and Sunday together."

"Sounds good to me." Grandma Harriet agreed. "I'll tell Paul. He'll be glad to hear it."

"Bye, Grandma."

"Bye, sweetie."

As I hung up the phone, I smiled, thinking of the wonderful time I would have visiting with Grandma Harriet and Paul. Little did I know how different that weekend would be from the pleasant visit I imagined.

CHAPTER TWO

I pulled into Grandma's driveway Friday. As I went inside, my overnight bag slung over my shoulder, I found her waiting in her rocking chair in the living room—same as always. "Hi, Grandma!" I greeted her with a huge grin and a gentle hug.

"Hello, sweetie."

"Is that Miss Tricia I hear in there?" a voice came from the kitchen.

"Of course," Grandma called back. "Come in here and see her, Paul."

Paul appeared from the kitchen, wearing an old paint-stained Minnesota Vikings sweatshirt—his favorite for working around the house. I immediately moved to give him a hug.

"Paul was fixing my sink for me," Grandma explained.

"What was wrong with your sink?"

"Nothing." She smiled.

About what I figured—Paul had been as eager to see me as Grandma had. "Looks like it's gonna be a good game tonight," I said. "True, we beat Jackson every year, but it looks like they might actually have a team this year."

"Paul's refereeing tonight," Grandma announced.

I gave him a speculative look. "At least I know the calls will be fair," I said.

He smiled. "No bad calls. And just between you and me, I hope Judsonville *does* win." He glanced down at his watch. "Hate to break this reunion short, but I have to get ready."

Grandma nodded.

"See you after the game, Paul," I added.

"Not right after," he said as he moved toward the door. "I have a stop to make after the game, and I don't know how long it will take. I might be a while."

"If all else fails, I'll see you tomorrow then," I countered.

"Sure thing, Tricia," he laughed as he pulled open the door. "Assuming that I'm still alive tomorrow, I'll see you then."

Later that Friday night I was in my truck again, heading back to school. Just about everyone who lived in Judsonville (and even some traitors from Stockton and the opposing fans of Bucknersville) was headed to Walter Camp Field. This was the night of the long-awaited Homecoming game. Football was definitely the biggest thing in Judsonville, and we all loved our Carrier High Mustangs.

I was about an hour early for the game—I'd planned it that way so I could get a good parking space. The parking lot was more-or-less empty, so I parked in the usual space. Since I was so early, I figured that I might as well get some studying done. I rolled down my window and picked up my Spanish book on the seat beside me.

I looked up as I heard another vehicle pull into the parking lot. My heart gave a little lurch. Luke was pulling into his regular space, to the left of mine. I buried my face in my Spanish book and heard Luke get out of his truck.

I expected him to leave without so much as a glance in my direction, but the next thing I knew, his face appeared in my truck window. "Hey, Tricia."

I looked up with genuine surprise. "Hi, Luke," I replied with a self-conscious smile. I wanted to smack myself for even caring what my stupid smile looked like.

"Spanish?"

"Yeah," I laughed. "My average is way less than perfect in there."

"Mine too," he admitted. Yeah, right. As if a 97 was a horrible average. Luke made me sick as far as Spanish was concerned.

"Would you like to head on in?" he asked.

"Um, I guess I could," I replied, tossing my book onto the seat beside me, wondering why he was bothering to wait for me. I hopped out of the truck, rolled up the window, grabbed my jacket and keys, locked the door, and shut it behind me.

"Do you already have your ticket?" he asked, gesturing to the stadium's side gate.

"No. I need to go up to the front gate and buy one." He didn't say anything else, but instead of crossing the street to the side gate, he kept walking beside me. "Do you think we'll win tonight?" I asked awkwardly.

"We'd better!" he replied. "We've never lost to Jackson! Kicking their tails in football every year is the only thing that makes their bad jokes tolerable."

"Yeah," I agreed. "Hopefully it'll be a pretty good game."

We were crossing the street to the front gate by then, and I heard a voice calling from the other side of the fence. "Hey, Luke!" It was a group of his friends, already inside.

"Hey!" Luke called back. "Well, Tricia, I guess I'll see you later," he said, heading for the gate.

"See you later," I said as he went to join his friends. I stepped up to the ticket window. I was all but floating on air, and once again, there was no good reason why.

By the fourth quarter we were behind by a field goal. This was unreal! We never lost to Jackson! The Mustangs bravely lined up against the line of scrimmage. It was second down, and the first down was merely four yards away.

I held my breath. The ball was snapped. The field was streaked with flashes of blue as the players flew into motion. Steve Johnson, number 10, took two steps backward, pulled back his arm, and courageously launched the ball into the air. A blue form that carried the number 3 broke through the confusion on the line of scrimmage and darted downfield, on a collision course with Steve's spiraling pass.

A green Bulldog jersey closed fast, but another blue one was gaining on him. The Bulldog reached for Jared Hutchins, the receiver. The ball came closer. The blinding white number 99 glared at me as the other blue jersey came from behind. My breath caught in my throat as Aaron's fingers closed around the Bulldog's jersey. . . .

"Aaron!" I whispered. "No. . . ."

The spiteful ball shot through Jared's open hands and slammed to the turf with a sick thud.

"No!" I shrieked.

The Bulldog hit the ground followed by Aaron, who still held a large handful of the green jersey in his fist. I watched in stunned disbelief as the referee, none other than Paul, walked to the center of the field and made a signal with his hands. I wasn't well-versed in football signals, but I didn't even have to guess what this one meant. I already knew—I had seen Aaron commit the sin with my own eyes.

The announcer's voice blared over the loudspeaker. "Holding, on the offense. Ten-yard penalty."

I was absolutely disgusted. The Mustangs marched back ten yards to try again, this time at second and fourteen instead of second and four. Aaron trotted a bit behind the others. I sighed as I watched him take his place on the new line of scrimmage. Everyone makes mistakes, but not everyone is unlucky enough to do it at a Homecoming game when his team is losing. Bummer.

The players jumped into motion again. Steve hurled the ball into the air. This one found its mark as number 48, Tim Ketron, snatched it out of the air, running like there was no tomorrow. A furious Bulldog plowed him into the ground, but the play had given us back the ten yards we had lost. Third down and four yards to go.

Standing just past midfield at the forty-two yard line, the goal must have still looked terribly far away as the Mustangs lined up. The two teams crouched motionless, staring each other down. I saw the movement on the line. Before I knew what had happened, both Aaron and his defender had crossed the line of scrimmage, yellow flags were flying everywhere, and the ball had never left the turf. The Mustangs were pointing accusingly at the Bulldogs as both sides stood up. It was impossible to determine who had moved first, but everyone seemed to think that it was the Jackson Bulldogs. I wasn't sure.

After a few moments of intense discussion with the other officials, Paul moved to the center of the field and made another unfamiliar gesture. I waited impatiently for the announcer. "Dead ball foul," he announced. "False start on the offense. Five yard penalty."

"What?!" I screamed. For a moment I forgot that it was my friend Paul on the field.

I saw Aaron march furiously up to Paul as the referee headed back toward the sidelines. I wasn't sure exactly what Aaron was saying, but I could tell that the words "He moved first" came out several times. Paul pointed a warning finger toward the field, and Aaron, not looking for a fight, nodded curtly and stalked back to the field.

The next thing I knew, Steve was being slammed to the dirt for a loss. Moments later there was a huge pileup on the field, short of the forty yard line and first down. The Mustangs had lost their fourth down gamble with only a minute left on the clock and no chance at redemption.

* * *

The next morning I climbed out of bed, feeling much better than I had the night before. It really stunk that we had lost to Jackson—on Homecoming—but the season itself hadn't really been damaged. As long as we made it into the playoffs, we could still be state champs. I was actually feeling okay about the whole thing by the time I got dressed.

I was whistling cheerfully as I walked through the hall of Grandma's house toward the living room. I stopped short, and the tune died on my lips. Grandma Harriet was sitting in her chair, crying her eyes out. "Grandma?" I asked, shaken. "What's wrong?"

"It's Paul," she managed between sobs.

I stared at her. "What about Paul?"

"He's dead," she sniffled.

My stomach gave a sickening lurch. "Dead?" I mumbled.

"Murdered!" Grandma erupted into a fresh bout of sobbing.

"Paul? Murdered?"

Grandma Harriet pointed to the morning paper. I snatched it off the coffee table. My eyes scanned the article. I read in disbelief about how the body had been found in the men's bathroom of the stadium. Paul's throat had been slashed, it said.

I stared in disbelief. Why in the world would anyone want to murder Paul, of all people? Something definitely didn't smell right.

Only one thought was running through my head as I got into my truck and backed out of Grandma Harriet's driveway—I had to get away, away from her sobs, away from the stark reality of my dear friend Paul's death. I drove in a daze, not really knowing where I was going. I was a bit surprised when I found myself parking my truck in my regular space at Carrier High.

The pathway between the fence and the back of the stadium was crawling with cops and who knows what other people. All sorts of vehicles were scattered in the parking lot—police black-and-whites, vans with nearly any profession imaginable short of pest control painted on the sides, unmarked cars with blue lights resting on the dashboards, and even a few nondescript vehicles that seemed absolutely normal.

Out of the corner of my eye, I saw a truck pull in next to mine. I turned, almost expecting Luke's gray Chevy, but it was Steve Johnson in his black Ford Ranger. I hastily climbed out of my Toyota and walked over to Steve's truck as he opened the door. He wore baggy jeans and a wrinkled tee shirt that looked like he had slept in them, and he didn't look like he felt very well this morning.

"What's going on?" I asked.

"You haven't heard?"

"About the murder, yes. But what are *you* doing here?"

"Coach called an emergency meeting this morning. He told us to be at the field house by eleven." Steve glanced at his watch. "Looks like I'm a couple minutes early." He looked up. "What are *you* doing here?"

"Just passing through," I replied. "Do you think your meeting's about the killing?"

He shrugged. "Probably. My guess is that the cops are going to ask us a few questions. Not that we would know anything, but in the movies they always ask everyone near the scene."

"That would be a lot of people," I said. "Considering all the fans at that Homecoming game last night. Besides, Steve, this isn't the movies."

"True, but I figure it's something about the dead guy. I certainly hope Coach didn't just call us out here to yell some more. He did enough of that last night."

"Why did he yell at you guys? If you did your best, that's all that matters."

"To tell the truth, he was yelling at himself as much as he was at us. He was pretty mad, and I think it was because of something more than the simple fact that we lost a game. It's just one loss, after all. We can still make playoffs, no problem."

"Then why would he get so upset?" I wondered. "Because it was Homecoming, or because we lost to Jackson, or what?"

Steve shrugged again. "Who knows? But I'd better head over to the field house."

"Steve?" I stopped him. "Would you do me a huge favor?"

"Like what?" he asked me suspiciously.

"Tell me what happens in your meeting."

"Why, Tricia?"

"Because . . . look, Steve. You know that guy who got killed? He was a good friend of mine—my Grandma's next-door neighbor. I just want to know what they tell you guys, and what they ask you. They can't give details in the paper, so I want to know what's really going on. There's no harm in that. You can do that for me, can't you, Steve?"

He gave me an uneasy look.

"Come on, Steve. They wouldn't tell you guys anything confidential anyway. Paul was my friend. I have to know what happened to him, and the only way to find out is to know what they know." I gestured to the people milling about behind the stadium. "And that starts with what they tell you." I looked him straight in the eye. "Steve, have I ever lied to you, or tried to deceive you ever in my life?"

"Not unless you count the time you told me that Erika Fisher had a crush on me."

I blushed. "She really did—honest."

"Whatever."

"Will you do this for me, Steve? It's more important than you know."

He sighed. "Okay, Tricia. Coach said that we wouldn't be all that long."

"I'll meet you after you get out. I have to run home, but I should only be a half-hour at most. If I'm not here, I will be in a few minutes, so wait on me."

Mom was at work, and the house was deserted when I got home. I was an only child, and Dad had died nearly two years ago, leaving just Mom and me. I had gotten used to coming home to an empty house, but today it seemed eerie.

I headed to my room, grabbed a handful of money from the stash in my dresser drawer, and crammed it into my pocket. I had a feeling that I was going to need gas before I was done driving around today.

I made my way to the kitchen to grab something to eat. I left the house with a sandwich, a bottle of water, and a bag of chips, which I dumped through the open window of my truck. Then I walked down the driveway to check the mail.

Across the street, my new neighbor was trying unsuccessfully to put up his mailbox. I could read the shiny, perfect black letters on the side which read: WHITMAN, 286-A HORIZON DRIVE. I had to admit that he was cute, but I definitely didn't think he was worth the fuss that Melissa and Rachael made over him. He couldn't even put up his own mailbox, for heaven's sake.

Waiting was pure agony. I needed to know what was going on, and sitting alone in the school parking lot with my overactive imagination wasn't my idea of comfort.

Most of the people in the stadium had left already and the remaining few were starting to dribble out, ducking under the yellow CAUTION, POLICE LINE tape that stretched from either end of the stadium to the fence. The side gate had been locked and the front one would probably be locked as soon as everyone finally left.

I noticed a group of guys walking through the front gate— they were the football players. They scattered to their vehicles. Steve walked toward my truck. He didn't look happy at all. In fact, all of the guys looked decidedly somber—they seemed in a hurry to leave. I had a very bad feeling about this. He walked up to my open window.

"It was about the murder, wasn't it," I said. It wasn't a question.

Steve nodded.

"What happened?" I asked.

"This guy, Sam Buckson, came in and said he was in charge of the investigation. He started off by giving us some spiel about how this killing was a serious thing, and how cold-blooded murders just don't happen around here. After he finished his speech he asked us if any of us knew Paul Sanders personally, but no one did. Then he held up a plastic bag with a bloody pocketknife in it. He asked if any of us had ever seen it before." Steve stopped, obviously upset.

"Did anyone say they had?" I prompted.

Steve nodded uneasily.

"Who?"

Steve looked up at me. "Aaron Tyler," he replied shakily. "It's his knife.

CHAPTER THREE

Monday morning I found myself slinging my overnight bag over my shoulder and promising Grandma Harriet that I would come back to visit soon. Between Grandma's crying and my dark brooding about the circumstances of the murder and what was going to happen to Aaron, this visit hadn't gone well at all. I escaped to my truck, backed out of the driveway, and cruised down the street at a restrained and legal thirty miles per hour when I would much rather have been doing sixty.

Judsonville didn't appear at all cheerful that morning. The junky cars at old Roscoe Thompson's place almost seemed to leer at me as I drove by. I supposed that part of that perception arose from my own gloomy thoughts, but there was no mistaking the fact that no one I saw was smiling.

I pulled into the parking lot and glowered at the unfamiliar car parked in my space. I sighed and hunted up another parking space, a lot farther from the school building than mine.

As the day progressed, it became painfully obvious how many things had changed because of Paul's murder. Poor Mrs. Tate, our principal, was nearly beside herself. Rowdy boys and fistfights she could handle, but murder was something completely different.

There was an assembly during first block during which Investigator Sam Buckson assured us Judsonville was still a safe place to live and that this murder was just a random event that could have happened anywhere—blah, blah, blah. I listened to the pointless speech critically—I was pretty annoyed with Mr. Buckson for being the guilty party responsible for taking my parking place. Investigator Buckson concluded by saying if we knew anything at all about Paul's death or had seen anything suspicious at the game that we should speak to him immediately. He must have been desperate for clues if he was asking us for help.

The only good thing that came out of the morning was that

after we returned to class, we had to listen to only about half of Mr. Burton's lecture about the assassination of President Lincoln—a slightly inappropriate topic, I thought, considering the circumstances.

During lunch, I found Aaron sitting alone at a small table in the cafeteria. I noticed that the guys who usually sat with him were eating at another table. I couldn't be sure if they had avoided him or if he had wanted to be alone. At any rate, I screwed up my courage, passed my normal table without a pause, and approached him. "Hello Aaron," I greeted him with a smile.

He looked up, surprised. "Hello, Tricia."

"Would you care for some company?" I asked.

He nodded. "Yes, I think so."

I sat down. "Jackie's not here today is she?" I asked. "I haven't seen her."

"No. She caught cold at the Homecoming game. And all of this trouble isn't helping matters any." He sighed. "I suppose you've heard about my knife. Most everyone has. I suppose half of them actually think I did it."

If there was one thing I knew about Aaron Tyler, it was that he was not a murderer. "I know you didn't do it, Aaron."

"I wish everyone believed in me that much," he sighed. "This is pretty tough, you know. Your own friends start to suspect you. None of them but Joe will even talk to me anymore without acting like they're about to wet their pants."

"They don't actually think you did it, do they?" I asked, gesturing to the guys at a table across the cafeteria. I saw Joe Taylor, Aaron's best friend, watching us from across the cafeteria. He had an odd, weary expression on his face.

"They don't know what to think."

"But surely they wouldn't think that of you. They know you." I glanced back over at Joe. Maybe he was weary of arguing with the guys on Aaron's behalf. . . .

"Yeah, but they know about my dad, too."

I stared at him blankly. "Your dad?"

"Very few people know this, but the reason that my dad's not around is because he's in jail. He shot and killed his boss in a blind rage when I was eight. Mom never would tell me why he did it—I still don't know. All I remember is that no one would ever so much as look at me and Mom again without suspicion back home in Maryland, so we moved down here that spring. Only my close friends know about it, and I guess they figure that if Dad could kill in a blind rage, then I could, too."

"Yeah, but why would you want to kill Paul Sanders? No one would get that upset over one questionable call."

"Yeah, but it wasn't just that one foul. The cops are also taking into account the holding call which I admitted was my fault. Plus, there were scouts there to watch me Friday night. They have to examine the possibility that I killed Paul Sanders because he made me look bad in front of those scouts."

"That's stupid!"

Aaron's voice was surprisingly calm. "They're just doing their job, Tricia."

"How did the killer get your knife, Aaron?" I asked.

He shrugged. "I don't know. I always carry my pocketknife with me, and I like to keep it good and sharp. A dull pocketknife's no good, you know. Anyway, I usually take it out of my pocket before heading back to the field house on Fridays, but I forgot it this time. I left it hanging on a hook in my locker where I'd be able to see it before I left. I suppose anyone could have come in and taken it, but no one was supposed to be in the field house."

"So what's the deal?" I asked. "Are you the prime suspect?"

"My guess is that I'm the *only* suspect."

It was then that I made a firm decision to see this through to the end and make sure that things turned around and came out right. I looked up. "I don't know if you knew this, but Paul Sanders was a very good friend of mine, like a brother. I need to know why he had to die. And I'm not going to have you blamed for something you didn't do. I mean look at this." I gestured to the table of Aaron's supposed friends. "This is stupid. Something needs to be done."

"Come on, Tricia," Aaron protested. "If the cops are stumped, what makes you think that you'll do any better?"

I smiled. "When I start asking questions, people don't immediately get suspicious. You never know what someone will let slip in front of a kid."

"You're going to get yourself into trouble," Aaron warned. "You don't have to do this for me."

I shrugged. "I'm not doing it for *you*, Aaron. I'm doing it for *me*. I have to know."

He sighed. "I'm not going to be able to make you change your mind and leave this to the cops, am I, Tricia?"

I smiled sweetly. "Fat chance."

He grinned at me. "Then good luck."

"Thanks," I replied. "I'm sure I'll need it before it's over."

Luke's penetrating glances were about to kill me. We were supposed to be writing skits in Spanish with a partner, but Mrs. Darwin was out of the room and there was much more talking going on than writing. Usually this dramatic stuff came pretty easily to me, but I couldn't concentrate with Luke burning a hole in my forehead with those stares of his. "What are you thinking?" I finally asked him.

"Lots of things," he mumbled.

"And I'll bet none of them have anything to do with Spanish."

"Nope." He paused for a moment. "Tricia, everyone has been treating Aaron so differently since they found out that it was his knife. That doesn't mean that he was the killer. Why is everyone so hasty to judge?"

"I don't know," I replied.

"What's it going to take to prove it to them? Does someone else have to be convicted before they'll come to their senses?"

I shrugged. "Who knows?"

"I mean, he's supposed to be popular, right? Think what would happen if the knife belonged to you or me. We'd probably be in jail by now."

"No one ever said that people were logical, or even overly bright."

"Yeah, but that's not fair to Aaron."

I looked up sharply. "I didn't know you knew Aaron."

"Well, I don't really," Luke admitted. "The truth is, he probably doesn't even know who I am, but he always seemed like a pretty nice guy."

"Yeah," I agreed. "He is."

"Wish I knew who really killed that ref," Luke said thoughtfully. "I hate it when a good guy's life gets screwed up for no good reason. I think the truth needs to come out—soon."

"Yeah, me too."

Luke looked up. "Why don't we find out?" he asked. "We could, you know."

"What are you talking about?"

"Why don't you and I find out who killed him? We both want to know, we'd be righting a wrong, and maybe we'd get a little more respect around here if we actually solved this."

I felt like telling him what a stupid idea that was, but how could I? I was already planning to do the same thing anyway! My pride asserted that I didn't need any help with this, but my brain insisted that I did. Who knew when I might need a little backup? Besides, I trusted Luke.

"All right," I agreed, actually relieved that I wasn't going into this alone. "But we shouldn't tell anyone about this."

"Deal," Luke said, thrusting out his hand. I shook it solemnly.

"Tricia, I really don't think that this is a very good idea," Luke protested from the passenger's seat as we drove toward Stockton after school.

"Have you got a better one?"

"Well, no, but—"

"Look, Luke. We want clues, and the logical place to find them is in Paul's house. I suppose if you're getting cold feet I could always turn around, take you back to your little gray Chevy, and do this by myself."

Luke looked hurt. "That was a spiteful thing to say."

"Sorry. Impatience is doing a number on me. But you're going to have to learn to trust me." I raised an eyebrow that my windshield could see but Luke couldn't. "You *do* trust me, don't you, Luke?"

He sighed. "Against my better judgment, yes."

"Then believe me when I say that we're going to be fine." I laughed softly. "Luke, have you done anything even remotely rebellious or exciting in your entire life?"

"Have you?" he shot back.

"No, not really."

"Then we're even." He looked up suddenly. "Wait a minute. We're not going to break in, are we?"

"Of course not. Grandma Harriet has a key."

"Don't you think she would protest your snooping around Paul's house?"

"Grandma doesn't talk in her sleep," I replied with a perfectly straight face as I glanced at my watch. "And she won't wake up from her afternoon nap for at least another hour." With that, I flipped on my blinker and turned into Grandma's driveway.

Luke gave me a hard look as I turned off my truck and dumped the keys in my pocket. "I'm trusting you, Tricia Lakely," he said sternly.

"Good," I replied with a bright smile. "Wait here."

I carefully opened the screen door, turned the knob, and stepped into Grandma's house. Her keys hung on little pegs just inside the door—all I had to do was lift the proper key from its peg and slip back out the door. I hooked the key ring on my pinkie, held it up to catch the light, and graced Luke with an extravagant bow followed by an impudent "Ta-da!"

He clapped his hands unenthusiastically. "After you," he offered dryly, gesturing to the sidewalk. I marched up to Paul's front porch, thrust the key into the lock, turned it, and opened the door.

"What exactly are we looking for?" Luke whispered as he quietly shut the door behind him.

"Relax. Nobody's going to hear you. We're looking for clues. Anything that looks suspicious."

"This guy was really organized," Luke said, looking around.

"Tell me about it," I replied. "Did you see his roses outside? Perfect. I don't know how he could be so neat. I'd say the cops haven't combed this place as much as they're going to, so try not to move anything or leave any prints. We don't want them to know that we've been here."

"Would we get in trouble if they found out?" Luke asked nervously.

"I don't know. But as long as we're careful they won't find out. Don't worry."

"I'll check out the living room, Tricia. You take the kitchen."

At first glance, the kitchen looked perfectly normal. I took a deep breath and tried to think of where I should start. I remembered that on TV they always looked for an address book so they could find out who the victim was associated with. I decided to look for that first. I didn't have any luck—either Paul didn't keep one, or the cops had taken it.

Just in case he had some numbers elsewhere, I pulled out his phone book. I opened to the first page, and, sure enough, a tiny piece of paper fluttered out. Lettered in neat handwriting were the letters *RT* followed by the number *555-1596*. The *555* meant that it was a Judsonville phone number, but I had no idea what

RT stood for, or whose number it was.

I grabbed a black permanent marker next to the phone, pulled up my left shirt sleeve, and wrote the letters *RT* and the number on my arm. Then I carefully put the slip of paper back into the phone book and slid it back into place for the cops to find—hopefully.

My search through the cabinets turned up nothing more than the usual pots and pans. I turned to the refrigerator. A calendar and a few ceramic magnets clung to the door. I was about to turn away when I caught sight of a little slip of paper. The blue lettering read: *286AHD*.

I stared at it, bewildered. The stars indicated that the message was important, perhaps a reminder, but what on earth did that gibberish mean? At first I thought it might be a license plate number, but then I remembered that the letters always come before the numbers on those. I sighed, picked up the black marker, and added this message beneath the phone number on my arm.

I quickly looked into the stove, the dishwasher, and the refrigerator. After finding nothing interesting at all there, I decided that I was done and moved into the living room to see how Luke was doing. I found him in the corner, his eyes glued to Paul's bulletin board. The square of cork was covered with neatly pinned newspaper articles, mostly about football. "Find anything?" I asked.

"I don't know," Luke replied. He pointed to an article with a headline that read: COLLEGE HEAD COACH ANNOUNCES RETIREMENT.

"Oh," I replied. "That's about Paul's favorite college team. They're a little school and not really up with the big dogs, but he always liked them. Their head coach is retiring after this season. Paul seemed to think that some of the ambitious high school head coaches have a shot at this one." I shrugged. "I don't know."

At that precise moment, Luke and I both nearly jumped out of our skins. Someone was fiddling with the doorknob . . . then a key slid into the lock. Luke's face was growing whiter by the second as I grabbed his arm and dragged him through the doorway into Paul's bedroom. I shut the door behind me with a barely audible click and desperately looked about for someplace to hide.

I opened the closet and looked inside. There was no place

for anyone in there. I started to panic. Luke looked like he was about to pass out. Frantically, I dropped to my hands and knees, lifted up the huge queen-size comforter on Paul's full-size bed, and slid under, dragging Luke after me—it was a good thing the bed was tall. The comforter was bunched against the floor, and I was afraid that if I leaned on it the bulge would be visible from the outside. "Scoot over!" I hissed at Luke.

"I can't!" he protested softly. "Not without lying on the comforter."

I bit back a very unladylike curse and tried to move away from the comforter. It wasn't working. That stupid comforter was taking up too much space for Luke and me to lie side by side under the bed without either one of us leaning against it. I heard the faintest of rustles as Luke moved, and the next thing I knew, we weren't on our backs anymore, and neither one of us was touching the comforter at all. Instead, Luke had rolled over on his side to face me, and put his arms about me, pulling me close to him. The sound of footsteps approaching the bedroom headed off my blush as I buried my face against Luke's chest, trying not to breathe.

"You check the kitchen, Tommy," a masculine voice said. The bedroom door opened.

"Whatever you say, boss," another voice—also male—replied from somewhere else in the house.

The man in the bedroom walked around. I could hear him open the closet door and start rummaging through the clutter inside. Paul's house looked neat on the inside, but his closet had suggested that even *he* had a sloppy side hidden away where no one could see it.

Had I opened my eyes I probably could have seen the man's shoes moving about the room through the tiny crack between the edge of the comforter and the wall the bed rested against, but I refused to move. I simply slid my arms around Luke's back and held him even tighter, feeling as if his warmth could melt away all of my fear.

"Come here, Tommy," the man in the bedroom called. I heard the footsteps enter the room and head toward the closet.

"Find anything, Sam?"

Sam. The name rang in my head like a fire alarm. Investigator Sam Buckson.

"Just a bunch of junk," Sam replied. "There's a lot of stuff in this closet. Why don't you help me go through it?"

"Sure," Tommy replied. I heard him kneel down.

"Did you find anything else in the kitchen?"

"Not really," Tommy replied. "But we looked it over quite a bit last time."

"Did you find any other phone numbers or anything written anywhere?"

"No," Tommy replied. "But we got his address book last time. The guys back at the office went through it, and it was nothing but family and neighbors and the sort. Nothing suspicious in the least."

"Hmm," Sam muttered.

"I did find one number, though. It was something hanging on the refrigerator. It's pure gibberish though—just a bunch of letters and numbers. You should come look at it before you leave. Other than that, I didn't really run across any addresses or numbers or anything like that unless you count the phone book. I kinda flipped through the pages, but I didn't see anything."

Duh, that was because the slip of paper was between the cover and the first page. If he just picked up the book, flipped through the middle, and never actually pulled the front cover away from the first page, he'd never find that slip of paper.

"Come on, Tommy," Sam said sarcastically, "*I've* got a phone book."

Tommy laughed. "I know." There was a pause before Tommy added, "There's a lot of stuff in here, isn't there?"

"Yeah," Sam replied. "Surprising for a guy who appeared to be such a neat freak."

"You don't suppose. . ." Tommy trailed off.

". . . that someone was rummaging around in here before us?" Sam finished. "I suppose anything's possible."

But I knew better. I remembered when Grandma Harriet had asked Paul once if there was ever anything out of place anywhere on his property. He had laughed and admitted ruefully that there was in his closet. That was the edge I had over the police—I knew Paul.

"You know, Tommy," Sam continued. "I think we should give this place another good combing. I had only planned on a couple of minutes here, you know. This is going to take longer than I'd planned, so I ought to stop by home, grab a bite to eat, and let Margaret know where I am."

"Yeah," Tommy agreed. "I'd like to say hi to Mary and the kids, too."

"Well then, let's go," Sam decided. "It's been a long day, and my stomach's growling." I heard a chuckle as the sound of the footsteps moved away. I lay motionless, waiting for the front door to click shut. I could feel Luke's muscles relax as we heard a vehicle start up outside.

I lay still for several more moments until the sounds of the engine trailed away before I almost reluctantly loosed my hold on Luke and felt his arms slide away from my back. I crawled out from under the bed, smoothed the comforter back into place, and hurried from the room.

I didn't even think to look back to see if Luke was following. He didn't pass me until I was out the back door and turning back to lock it. We headed straight for the fence and didn't so much as breathe until we were beside my truck.

"Well, that was, uh, interesting," Luke said, grinning.

I burst out laughing, gasping for breath at the same time. I was feeling a bit giddy at the moment. "Didn't I warn you? Stay here a sec." I sprinted back up to Grandma's porch, cracked open the door, replaced the key, and noiselessly shut the door behind me. Then I walked back to the truck, opened the door, pulled my keys out of my pocket, and got in. "So, are you getting more than you bargained for yet?" I asked.

"Nah," he grinned as I turned on the ignition. "Didn't you know that hiding from cops under beds is my hobby?"

I turned serious again, glancing at my watch. "Your parents would have expected you home by now, wouldn't they?"

"And your mom wouldn't?" he shot back as he buckled his seat belt.

"Yeah, she would," I admitted. "Oh well. I guess if you insist, we can start breaking family rules together."

"Thanks, Tricia."

"For what?" I asked, confused.

He smiled. "For saving my tail." He leaned slowly toward me, but I turned away as if I hadn't noticed what he was trying to do.

I put my truck into gear. "Any time," I mumbled as I stepped on the gas, wondering if I should have kissed him.

CHAPTER FOUR

To this day I still don't know how in the world I got Mom to accept the lame story about my truck running out of gas. Maybe it was because I'd never really told her a lie about anything important. I felt terrible, but it couldn't be helped. I don't know how Luke fared, but he must have managed all right because he sounded fine when he called me later that evening. I didn't even think to ask him how he had gotten my number, and he didn't volunteer the information.

Luke and I had discussed the findings at Paul's on the way home, and it turned out that Luke hadn't come across anything much. He asked me about the closet—if the cops might have something with it—but I told him that Paul's closet hadn't been ransacked.

"So what about those numbers?" Luke prompted eagerly, referring to the two strange figures I had told him about on the way home. "Why couldn't you tell me what they were in the truck?"

"Because I can't read and drive at the same time."

"Well . . . ," he said impatiently after a couple of seconds. "Are you gonna tell me or not?"

"Wait a sec!" I protested. "I've got to roll up my sleeve first. I wrote them on my arm."

"Your arm?" he asked skeptically.

"Well, where would you have written it?" I shot back. "On your shirt?" He didn't have an answer for that. "Okay. I found the first one in Paul's phone book on a little slip of paper. It reads 'RT 555-1596.'"

"Sounds like a phone number."

"Yeah. A Judsonville number, too, but I have no idea whose it is."

"Don't know. . . ," Luke trailed off. "Well, we'll figure it out later. What was the other one?"

"286AHD," I replied. "I found it on the fridge with little stars drawn on either side of it."

"286AHD?" he repeated in bewilderment. "What on earth does that mean?"

I shook my head. "I have no idea."

"Why don't we both write this down now before you lose it in the shower," Luke suggested.

"How kind of you to realize that I really don't want to go a week without showering so that I can let that black marker rot into my arm!" I said sarcastically.

"Be nice, Tricia."

"Of course," I replied sweetly. "I'm always nice."

"Can you think of anything else, Aaron?" I asked, probably for the ten-millionth time.

"I don't know, Tricia. I was playing football at the time. Homecoming or no, everything beyond the grass on that field was just background noise to me."

I sighed. "And you have no idea what RT might stand for or what 286AHD is?"

"No. Sorry, Tricia. I wonder if Sam Buckson knows?"

"I don't know," I mused. "I'd give anything to know what he's thinking now or what he's up to."

"You sound like you don't trust him."

I shrugged. "I don't entirely. In this game, I suppose it's best not to trust someone until he gives you reason to. The murderer could be anyone in Judsonville and I haven't checked anyone off my list but me, you, and my partner. Not even my mom."

Aaron looked up quickly. "Partner? Tricia, are you sure that's a good i—"

"Of course it's a good idea," I jumped in. "It really isn't safe to undertake something like this alone, and—"

"It isn't safe, period, Tricia," Aaron interrupted. "I thought you said no one could be trusted—"

"I said not until he proved he could be."

"And how did this person prove it?"

"Never mind. Just believe me, Aaron. I trust Luke, and you probably should too."

"Well, he hasn't given *me* reason to tr— Luke?" he asked blankly.

"Yes, Luke," I replied defensively.

"You mean Luke *Benson*?"

"Yes, Luke Benson! What's wrong with him?"

"Well I. . . ," Aaron stammered. "Well, I, uh. . . ." He looked confused. "I don't know him. . . ."

"Exactly! That's why no one would suspect that he and I would be snooping into this murder. And that's what will keep us perfectly safe."

"Just for the record, I still think this whole thing is a bad idea," Aaron warned.

"And just for the record," I said with a wink, "I'm not listening."

"You know, Luke, if you don't shut up for a minute and let me finish writing this skit, we're both going to get F's."

Luke looked at me blankly. "What?"

"You know . . . no skit . . . F's. . . ."

"But this is important, Tricia. The skit's not due till—"

"Till the end of class!" I snapped.

"The end of class?" Luke blinked back into reality. "Are you serious?!"

"Would you like to bet your 97 average on it?"

"Why aren't we done yet?" Luke babbled.

"Because you won't shut up long enough to let me write a single word," I growled, "much less a coherent sentence." I began to scribble with a renewed vigor. Almost done. . . .

"You know, Tricia—"

I stubbornly tuned him out, determined to complete my task before he could distract me again. Only a few more sentences. . . .

"That name rings a bell somewhere. I feel like I ought to know it." I tried to ignore him, but my curiosity whittled away at my resolve, and finally I gave in.

"All right, I surrender," I sighed. "What name?"

"Tommy," Luke replied. "It seems so familiar."

I shrugged. "It's a pretty common name."

"Yeah, but I know I've heard it somewhere before."

"Hmm," I replied. My hand started moving again. "Luke?"

"What?" He looked up eagerly.

"Look up 'to spill' for me."

Luke looked disappointed. "I thought it was something important."

"It is."

"Well, you know what I meant." He picked up the Spanish dictionary and started flipping through it. "So what are you spilling, Tricia?"

"Your blood if you don't find that word."

He laughed. "Here it is."

He handed me the book and I wrote the desired word on the page. "Done," I announced triumphantly, just as the bell rang.

"It's about time," Luke said. I gave him an evil look. "All right, all right," he laughed. "I'll shut up."

"Get your books," I said as I slung my backpack over my shoulder and shut my truck door.

"What for?" Luke asked.

"Because we're supposed to be studying, remember?" I replied.

"Oh yeah." Luke grabbed his books and slammed the door behind him.

"Come on." I took a deep breath as I reached for the door-knob. I'd never brought a guy home with me before. I wasn't sure how Mom was going to take it. I stepped inside and stopped short. She wasn't alone. She was sitting at the kitchen table with a cookie in her hand, laughing. Across from her sat the new guy from across the street.

Mom looked up, surprised. "Hi, sweetie." She gestured at him. "This is Mr. Francis Whitman from across the street."

I graced them with a fake smile. "Hi, Mr. Whitman."

"Hello, Tricia," he replied cheerfully. "You can just call me Francis, if you like. Mr. Whitman is my father."

"Sure, Francis, no problem," I replied blankly, trying not to laugh at the most horrible attempt at a British accent I've ever heard.

I noticed that Mom was looking quizzically at Luke, who was uncomfortably shifting his weight from one foot to the other behind me. "This is Luke," I announced. "We're just going to go back and study," I said, gesturing down the hallway. Then I grabbed his hand and half dragged him down the hallway before Mom could say a word.

"Are you okay, Tricia?" Luke asked, giving me an odd look as I dumped my books on the floor and plopped down on my bed.

I snapped back into reality. "Fine. Why?"

He gave me one of those horrible, penetrating looks. "What's going on?"

I flinched. I couldn't lie to him when he looked at me like that. "I . . . I don't know," I sighed. "Something about Mom and Francis just sitting there. I mean he's so . . . so. . . ." Suddenly there just weren't any words.

"Young, good looking," Luke offered with a slight edge in his voice.

I shook my head. "No. That's not it at all. More like . . . helpless. I mean the guy couldn't even put up his own mailbox, and Mom was laughing with him. It's not really all that easy to charm my mother."

"Well," Luke offered, "I don't know about you, but if I were your mom I couldn't help but laugh at him. I mean, did you hear his accent? Where did he get it, from some cheesy soap opera?"

I laughed. "That's mean, Luke."

"Yeah, but that accent can't be natural. If he took that much time to learn it, he deserves to be laughed at. What's wrong with a good ol' Suthu'n accent?" he drawled.

I shrugged, took one look at Luke, and started laughing all over again. When I was finally able to stop the evil giggling, I shook my head and jumped into conversation before I could start again. "Anyway, back to the business at hand. Who would have a reason to kill Paul? He's such a nice guy."

"What did Paul do besides referee? Did he have a regular job?"

"Yeah. He was a delivery guy for Venny's Shipping Company."

"Hmm," Luke muttered. He sighed. "This is like chasing a needle in a haystack," he grumbled.

My eyes widened. "Wait a minute, Luke. What if we're going about this all wrong?"

He looked up. "What do you mean?"

"Anybody in Judsonville could have some hidden motive for killing Paul. I mean, he could have accidentally run over some old lady's pet chipmunk for all we know. Maybe we shouldn't be looking for someone who *would* have killed Paul, but someone who *could* have killed him."

"That doesn't narrow things down much, Tricia," Luke protested. "Just about all of Judsonville, and then some, was at that football game."

"But not all of them could have gotten their hands on Aaron's knife."

"Who would have had access to the field house?" Luke asked.

"I don't know, but I think I know someone who might."

"Hmm," Aaron said thoughtfully. "I don't know who could have gotten in, but I know who was supposed to be there."

Aaron, his best friend Joe Taylor, Luke, and I sat at a little round table in the cafeteria, almost in a separate world from the rest of the school. "You know," Aaron continued, "the coaches, the other guys, the water boys and the cheerleaders. Nobody else uses the field house this time of year. Besides, I left the knife in there right before the game. That means the cheerleaders weren't in there. And the rest of us were just there during halftime. It's possible but highly unlikely that anyone else would be able to sneak in unnoticed if they didn't belong." He looked at Joe. "Can you think of anyone else?"

"Not anyone game-related."

"It doesn't matter," I said promptly. "Anyone. Can you think of anyone at all?"

"Not unless you count the janitor," Joe replied.

My head snapped up. Luke and I shared a startled look as we said together, "The janitor? The janitor!"

By the expression Joe had on his face, he must have thought we were crazy. But Aaron knew me well enough to expect something like this. He'd already jumped ahead of us. "And nobody notices where the janitor goes. He has access to anything on the school grounds. There would be nothing strange about him going into the field house during the game."

Joe seemed a bit skeptical of the whole thing. "But why would the janitor want to kill a ref?" he asked.

I sighed. "I don't know."

Was Bobby Joe Fink capable of murder? He wasn't a very cheerful person, but still! He probably didn't even know Paul. No use in actively suspecting innocent bystanders—yet. All I knew was that this detective stuff was starting to get really complicated.

"Okay," Luke said, a puzzled look in his eyes. "Let's review what we know. We know that the football team, the coaches, the cheerleaders, the water boys, and the janitor have access to the field house. We know that 286AHD means something, but we don't know what. We also know that 555-1596 is a phone number, and we're assuming that RT is a person. We know that Paul Sanders had a ridiculously neat and clean house—except for the closet—and it hasn't been ransacked, because nothing's out of place."

"Pretty thin," I said glumly. "After all, it's like chasing shadows in the dark. I don't know anything about investigating a crime."

"It sounds like you've got as much as the police," Aaron said. "Probably more, since they're spending all their efforts looking for evidence to incriminate me." He sighed. "I'm surprised they haven't arrested me yet. It's only a matter of time I suppose."

"Do you have any kind of an alibi at all?" Luke asked.

"Sort of, but not really. The autopsy report indicated that Paul Sanders died sometime shortly after the game. Of course, I was still on the field right after the game ended. Before I went back to the field house, though, I ran out to the back parking lot through the back gate in the corner to get another roll of film out of my car. We'd been taking pictures before the game, and I wanted to take a couple more pictures before we left. All the guys were either on the field or heading back to the field house. Nobody was with me, and no one recalled seeing me leave and return. No one can witness that I didn't go back to the bathroom and kill Paul Sanders in that few minutes."

"Did they ever get the results back on the fingerprints on that knife?" I asked.

"They put a rush on it," Aaron replied, "but my attorney says it will still take time." He made a face. "Who ever thought I'd need a lawyer in high school? Mom and I are going to be in debt up to our ears before this is over."

A single glance at Luke's creased eyebrows told me that he wasn't thinking about pricey lawyers. "This doesn't add up," he finally said. "Why should they be so sure that Aaron did it? It could have just as easily have been the janitor, one of the other players, or even Coach Jones, for all they know. The fact that it was Aaron's knife doesn't mean anything. Anyone could have taken it from that field house. Why are they pouncing on Aaron like this?"

Aaron shook his head. "I don't know."

"Well, I've got a good guess," Joe spoke up. "They want a simple solution. Murders don't happen around here every day. They want something easy, something just like all the other domestic violence murders they work with. They don't want anyone to think that Judsonville has any kind of a darker side—that anyone would have a motive deeper than blind rage. Judsonville's a small, quiet town and they want to keep it that way."

"By convicting a high school student?" I demanded sharply. Sometimes I let my emotions carry me off a bit too far.

Joe shrugged. "If that's what it takes to keep order. All they have to do is make the incident with Aaron's dad public knowledge, and everyone will dismiss this as some kind of a family thing. A rare case. In two years, no one will remember it ever happened."

"Except for us," I protested. "How could we forget?"

"Tricia, they're not worried about us. In two years we'll all be graduated, and most of us will have moved far away from Judsonville."

I fought my way through my churning anger and regained my composure. This was taking things too far. . . . But that's why I was out to disprove their idiotic accusations, right? After all, practically no one in Judsonville made sense. Just think, if Roscoe Thompson was a loan shark, he'd have to be pretty nuts to do business in Judsonville—

An alarm went off in my head as that name jumped away from my rambling thoughts to stare me straight in the face. RT! Roscoe Thompson!

"Wait!" I exclaimed, a wild look flaring into my eyes. The others looked up at me, startled. "I need a phone book!"

Joe gave me a peculiar look. "A phone book? Tricia, what on earth does a phone book have to do with narrow-minded cops, the field house, or Paul's murder?"

"Just get me a phone book!" I babbled, trying to make my excitement-overloaded brain function properly again.

Luke raised one eyebrow. "I think she's onto something!"

Aaron jumped up out of his seat.

"Where are you going?" Joe asked.

"To get a phone book," Aaron called back over his shoulder.

I could almost feel the tension around the table as we waited. I could tell that Luke wanted to ask me what was going on, but he knew me well enough to understand that I couldn't put it into words just yet. I was incredibly relieved to see Aaron returning, the answer to my suspicion clutched in his hand as if he were carrying a football through the defensive line instead of a phone book across the cafeteria. He sat down quickly, then nervously handed me the phone book.

I took it eagerly and immediately started flipping through it. *Lucas* . . . no . . . I wanted *T* . . . there's *Taylor* . . . almost there . . . *Thompson.* My finger froze on the page and I took a deep breath as my eyes read the name once more to be sure: ROSCOE

THOMPSON, CARSON DRIVE.

I was almost afraid to look at the number, but I forced my eyes to move across the page. It took a moment for me to comprehend the numbers I was reading. I let the phone book slide from my fingers to thunk on the table as the other three stared at me impatiently. I took a deep breath to keep from screaming across the cafeteria. "It's him. . . ," I managed.

"What?" Joe asked, confused.

"Him?" Aaron shook his head.

But Luke knew what I was talking about. "Who?" he asked excitedly. "Who is it, Tricia?"

I threw a couple of furtive glances in either direction to make sure no one was paying attention to us before leaning forward and in low tones uttering the name "Roscoe Thompson."

"Roscoe Thompson?" Luke hissed.

I nodded.

"Roscoe Thompson?" Joe didn't have a clue what was going on. "What about him?"

"RT. The phone number," Aaron said suddenly. "It's his, isn't it?"

I nodded. "555-1596."

Aaron whistled. "So why did your Paul have Roscoe Thompson's phone number in his phone book?" he asked me.

I shook my head. "I haven't the slightest idea."

"Was he in need of a junky used car?" Joe asked doubtfully.

"No," I replied.

"Then I say something smells fishy," Luke said.

"I agree," Aaron added. "What if Roscoe Thompson really is a loan shark, and Paul owed him money? If he didn't pay, old Roscoe might have had him killed."

Luke shrugged. "It's pretty thin. But at this point, anything's possible."

"Either way," Aaron said, "we need to know why Paul had Roscoe's number."

"There's only one way to find out," I declared. I looked Luke straight in the eye and gave him a mischievous smile. "I think it's about time you go shopping for a used vehicle, Luke, don't you?"

CHAPTER FIVE

I leaned against the passenger window of Luke's truck, feeling rather nervous. I was dressed all in black to match the darkness of Roscoe Thompson's nasty place, and my dark hair was pulled into a bun. Luke was in old jeans and a flannel shirt that were supposed to give him the slob effect, but for some reason, they made him look more attractive.

"So what was your excuse this time?" I asked casually.

He shrugged. "I told them I was going to a late movie. I can get away with that every once in a while this time of year. You?"

"I said I was meeting someone at the movies," I admitted.

"Didn't she ask who you were meeting?" Luke asked curiously.

"Yes," I replied carefully.

"Who did you tell her?"

Sometimes he was awfully dense. I headed off a blush that was threatening to give me away. "I told her you were taking me." Luke gave me a startled look. "Come on, Luke. She would have gotten suspicious about us spending so much time together anyway. Mom's not stupid. And she would have been hurt if she thought we were going out and I didn't want to tell her."

All Luke could do was shrug. He seemed at a loss for words. He pulled off the road with seeming relief. I opened the door and stepped out of his truck. "Good luck," I said as I slammed the door shut. He grinned at me and drove away.

I sighed and disappeared into the underbrush alongside the road. Confusion would have to wait. Right now I didn't have the time to try to figure out Luke Benson. Believe me, that would really take time. Sometimes I wondered if it would ever be possible for me to understand him. I guess anything's possible, though. After all, if I could assume that it was possible to sneak into Roscoe Thompson's place and sneak out again without getting shot, why couldn't I assume it was possible to figure out Luke Benson? Both of them were pretty big ifs.

Roscoe Thompson's used car lot wasn't a very inviting place. Maybe the reputation added to the effect, but the eerie shadows cast by the big brick building and the leering stares of rows and rows of old beat-up cars alone were enough to make me think twice about going through with this. I steeled myself and took a deep breath as I peered through the thorn bushes and watched Luke get out of his truck.

Roscoe Thompson himself appeared from the ugly brick building that served as office and residence in one. I figured he must have some kind of a shady secret to want to hide it in that dark, ugly thing. I wondered how he could stand the place.

As Luke and Roscoe started up a conversation over the hood of a junky yellow Toyota, I crept out of the bushes and made for the closest car. I crouched low and scampered from car to car, moving toward the brick building.

I hesitated behind the car closest to my destination, staring apprehensively at the side door. As far as I knew, Roscoe lived alone, but there was nothing to assure me that no one else was there. I didn't want to run into another person in there—or even a junkyard Doberman, for that matter. I took a deep breath and decided that if I had come this far, I might as well keep trusting my luck.

I took a quick look around the bumper of the blue car. Roscoe's back was to me, and he and Luke appeared to be deep into a conversation. Luke caught my glance and in the split second before he turned away, something passed between us. I wasn't sure how I knew, but I was sure without a doubt that Luke wanted me to go now.

I took a deep breath and darted across the few yards of open space to the door. The door was still slightly ajar, so I gave it a nudge and slipped inside.

I scanned the room quickly. It appeared to be Roscoe's living room. It was a very large room with a polished wooden floor and a fireplace at one end. There were all the normal items: a couch, two wing chairs, a recliner, a television, a huge bookcase filled with massive old volumes, a tall grandfather clock, an empty coffee table, an end table that held only a lamp and book with eyeglasses resting on it, and two more tall lamps on the other side of the room.

Heavy curtains were drawn across the windows, and the only light came from the lamp on the table, probably on its lowest setting. The dim light made me feel like I was in the middle of an old Sherlock Holmes movie.

I still wasn't sure if I was alone, so I was careful not to make any noise as I tiptoed across the living room toward the door directly across from me. I reached out and cautiously brushed the doorknob with the tips of my fingers, almost as if I expected it to burn me. I closed my eyes, trying to tune out the frenzied thudding of my heart, as I grasped the knob and turned.

I opened the door the tiniest crack and peered inside. The kitchen was bathed in light. No one was there. As I passed through the door, it was like stepping into another dimension. While the living room reminded me of something out of an antique storybook, this brightly illuminated kitchen could have belonged in any house in Judsonville. The cream colored floor tiles and cheerful white walls calmed my fears, and I almost felt at home here.

I quickly reminded myself that I wasn't here to kill time and made my way through the kitchen, but nothing seemed out of the ordinary at all. I was basically running on the theory that Roscoe Thompson was a loan shark, and I doubted that a loan shark would keep important files in the kitchen anyway.

There were a total of three doors leading into the kitchen—I had come through one, and two were to my right. I took a quick step to the left, pulled the curtain back from a small window, and glanced outside to be certain that Luke still had Roscoe entertained. It seemed that they had waded waist-deep into some involved yet probably meaningless discussion over the hood of that old yellow Toyota.

I turned away from the window with a bit more confidence that Roscoe might not catch me after all and stared at the two doors. I pulled open the first door and peeked inside. It was the bathroom. Not finding anything useful, I shut the door and tried the second one.

This one led to a utility room. Roscoe's washer and dryer stood against one wall of the small room, and there were assorted piles of clothes on the floor or on the dryer or resting in overflowing laundry baskets strewn across the room. Typically male, I thought as I picked my way through the laundry piles to the door on the other side. It seemed that I should have run into some trouble by now. I half expected to find someone waiting for me in the room beyond as I held my breath and opened the door the tiniest crack.

I dared not breathe as I peered inside. My eye searched the room frantically, but no one was there. I let out a careful sigh of relief and stepped into Roscoe's bedroom. The sunlight pouring through the open blinds on the windows illuminated the room as I started poking about. The place wasn't meticulously organized like the living room, but it wasn't sloppy like the laundry room, either.

This may be a silly comparison, but like baby bear's bed, this room was "just right." And just like Goldilocks, I was sneaking around someone else's house looking for something "just right"—the right clue that would lead me to Paul's killer. I felt closer than ever, but there was nothing to prove I wasn't still miles and miles away.

I wandered through the bedroom, searching for something useful. What I was looking for was some kind of set of files or papers, but all I found were clothes and books and blankets and all the normal things one would expect to find in a bedroom. I took a quick look under the bed, but nothing was there. There weren't even any boxes stacked in the closet—nothing but the normal clothes and shoes.

This was getting me nowhere. I could see through the other two bedroom doors that I had covered the building—one led back the living room and the other to the tiny bathroom I had already seen and searched.

I was about to shut the closet door with disgust when I noticed something strange. In the very back corner of the closet sat some very peculiar shoes. They were wooden and looked very, very old. Cobwebs were forming across the backs of them, and they didn't look very used. Of course, I probably wouldn't wear old wooden shoes like that, either—they looked very uncomfortable. I wondered why in the world Roscoe Thompson would keep antique shoes he never wore in the back of his closet. Perhaps because he had no other place for them, I thought, but I decided to kneel down and take a look anyway.

I reached for the right shoe and tried to slide it toward me, but it wouldn't move. That was strange. The shoe may have been made of wood, but it didn't look all that heavy. I tugged again, this time on the left shoe, but it also refused to move. Deciding to try a different tactic, this time I tried to lift the right shoe instead. The shoe did move this time, but it did not come loose from the floor as I had expected it to. Instead, the heel moved up with my hand, but the toe remained firmly against the floor.

I nearly jumped out of my skin as I heard a soft movement. My head whipped up and I stared in astonishment as the back wall of the closet began to slide away from me. For a moment I feared that I was in the process of passing out, but the wall really was moving away. I gasped involuntarily and gave the wooden shoe a sharp look. Attached to the heel of the shoe was a tiny metal bar that must have triggered the wall to move when I pulled it out of the floor.

This was feeling more and more like the movies. I wouldn't have been a bit surprised to see Harrison Ford as Indiana Jones come strolling out of that opening, old leather jacket, beat-up hat, whip, and all. I cautiously rose to my feet, furtively glanced behind me, and slid through the new gap in the closet.

Before me lay a staircase, shrouded in shadow. My courage was running out, but I still had enough will left to force myself up those stairs and into the office above. This office was a stark, empty room with plain block walls. In the center stood a huge, elaborate oak desk with a very comfortable armchair behind it and a plain wooden chair in front. The windows were barred and covered. This place had obviously been designed for intimidation. I could hardly believe that there could actually be a loan shark in Judsonville, but the rumors were looking more and more true all the time.

I strolled straight past the desk and across the room to the front window. I picked up the bottom corner of the cardboard covering the window and peered outside. Good. Luke and Roscoe were still busy. The last thing I needed was for Roscoe to find me up here.

Actually, I had made my tour of the downstairs very quickly, and the townsfolk said that Roscoe was a talker when it came to cars. From bits and pieces I'd picked up from classmates' conversations, Luke wasn't ignorant on the topic himself.

I headed back to the desk and went for the middle drawer first. I pulled at the handle, but it wouldn't move—it was locked. Since I hadn't seen any business-related articles at all downstairs, and this empty room was all there was to the upstairs, logic told me that the files and the car keys had to be in this desk. If I wanted the keys to the drawers I was going to have to lure Roscoe Thompson up here.

I headed back down the stairs and out of the closet. For a moment I stared at the opening, wondering how in the world I was going to close it. There could have been a million different possibilities that Roscoe could have designed, but fortunately for me, he had picked an easy one. The very first thing I tried was pushing the heel of the wooden shoe back to the floor, and I sighed with relief as the wall moved back into the closet, where it was supposed to be.

I shut the closet door and headed for the living room. The windows faced the front of the building, and as I carefully pulled the bottom of the curtain away I could see Roscoe, still with his back to me.

I waved my hand until I was finally able to attract Luke's eye. I made a frenzied motion with my fists that was supposed to resemble steering a car. He looked away, and I wondered for a moment if he had understood the message. I should never have doubted him. As I pressed my ear to the glass, I was relieved to hear the plainly clear words, "Well, Mr. Thompson, sir, think I'll give this baby a bit of a test drive, what do you think?"

Luke's imitation of Francis Whitman's accent made me want to burst out laughing, but under the circumstances I didn't think it would be appropriate. Instead I quickly backed away from the window and dashed into the bedroom.

Suddenly I realized I needed to find a hiding place before Roscoe found me wandering around in his house. My eyes fell on a welcome object just in front of me, and I dropped to my knees and crawled into my familiar hiding place. It was strangely ironic that as Roscoe Thompson opened the door and stepped into his house, I found myself once again hiding from danger under a bed.

CHAPTER SIX

Roscoe Thompson clomped right past me and headed straight for the closet. I peered carefully at his feet from beneath the bed. Without even hesitating, he nudged the wooden shoe up with his foot. I muttered a silent prayer as I watched him head through the back wall and heard the sound of his footsteps going up the staircase.

As soon as he was gone I slid out from under the bed and crept back to the window. I yanked up the curtain and began to gesture wildly out the window at Luke. For this to work, Roscoe was going to have to be in enough of a hurry to leave his keys behind him. Luke raised an eyebrow and winked at me.

I flinched as he started bellowing curse words as if he were in severe pain. I wasn't implying the swearing, but some sort of loud diversion was what I had had in mind. Either Luke was beginning to read my mind or I was beginning to think like a male. Either idea was fairly startling.

It was then that I realized Roscoe Thompson would be coming back down those stairs fairly rapidly any second now, and I was out in plain view. I had nowhere to hide and no clue what to do. I was operating completely on instinct, and unfortunately instinct was failing me at the moment. It wasn't like me at all not to think ahead—maybe I *was* starting to think like a male. Scary thought.

I looked around frantically. I felt the color drain from my face and the adrenaline whirl inside me like a hurricane. My eyes fell on the wing chair next to the fireplace and I dashed behind it, just in time to hear the closet wall closing and Roscoe Thompson's approaching footsteps. I held my breath until he was safely outside. I still refused to move from my hiding place, even as I heard Luke explaining that he had hit his newly healed elbow (that he had never broken) on the car and that it hurt like, well, you-know-what. I listened tolerantly to the occasional four-letter words he threw in for effect. I was going to have to have a talk with him about that swearing, diversion or no.

I listened with relief as I heard two car doors open and close, rather than just one. It seemed that Luke might be taking Roscoe with him. Not a bad idea. I crawled almost reluctantly from behind the chair and cautiously peeked through the curtains as the yellow car puttered away. There were definitely two forms in that car. Roscoe was gone with Luke, and I had the house all to myself.

I certainly didn't have time to kill, so I hopped to my feet and ran back into the bedroom, abandoning all attempts at silence. I kicked up the wooden shoe, waited impatiently for the wall to move, and darted up the stairs.

I pulled the ring of tiny silver keys out of the keyhole in the small top drawer overflowing with car keys of all shapes and sizes. I tried the big drawer on the lower right side very first thing. It took me a minute to find the right key, but when I finally opened the drawer I was ready to squeal with delight. The drawer was chock-full of files; and with labels such as "overdue," "jobs for TJ," and "contacts," I rather doubted that they pertained to used cars.

I started thumbing through the files and stopped abruptly as my astonished eyes fell on the heading I was looking for: "Sanders, Paul." I could barely believe my eyes. How could Paul have been associated in any way with Roscoe Thompson? A loan shark? He must have been awfully desperate. I snatched up the file and opened it anxiously.

The first sheet appeared to be background information on Paul. His address and phone number were there, and his jobs as a deliveryman for Venny's and as a referee for the High School League. I skimmed past all the stuff I already knew and into the next paragraph. I read on in surprise as I stumbled across something I had never known before. The paper said that Paul had claimed he needed the loan to pay for his mother's cancer treatments. Unfortunately she had died in the hospital, and Paul was up to his ears in unpaid bills. This struck me as a complete surprise—Paul had never spoken of his mother.

The next sheet read the figures of Paul's debt. I whistled. That was a lot of money. He had paid most of it back, but he still had a few thousand to go. Still, judging by the figures, Paul had paid the original loan amount and was now working on interest. That meant that Roscoe Thompson hadn't lost any money. Why would he kill over a few thousand dollars? From the number of files in that drawer, I doubted that he was anywhere near bankruptcy.

I snatched a blank sheet of paper from the drawer and hastily copied the figures onto it before replacing the file. I was grateful that I didn't have to use my arm for a notepad this time as I wadded up the paper and stuffed it into my pocket.

I quickly shuffled through the other files, looking for any names I might recognize. All of Roscoe's debtors seemed to be from out of town, and that made perfect sense. I mean, how many people in tiny little Judsonville would actually be in need of a loan, much less a loan shark? My finger lingered on the very last file in the drawer. This name I knew. In fact, I saw the man every day. It was Bobby Joe Fink, the school janitor.

I was barely able to glance at the figures before I heard the car pulling back into the lot. I hastily shoved the file back into place and slammed the drawer shut. After carefully locking the drawer, I replaced the tiny silver key in the keyhole of the smaller, open drawer. Then I lit out of there, tore down the steps, stomped the wooden shoe, and slid back under the bed.

I wasn't sure how long I stayed under the bed before I heard Luke pull out of the lot and Roscoe come back inside. Everything was as he had left it, and all that was left was for me to hold my breath and wait for the right moment to escape. The minutes dragged by with agonizing slowness. All I wanted was to crawl out from under that bed, run like the blazes, and get out of there. But instead I lay motionless beneath bed—I wouldn't get more than four steps as long as Roscoe Thompson was planted in his living room.

It felt like an hour before I heard him move, even though a glance at my glow-in-the-dark watch said that it had been only fifteen minutes. I froze as Roscoe walked into the bedroom, but he didn't even slow down as he passed the bed. He headed straight for the bathroom, stepped inside, and shut the door behind him. I paused only a second before making the decision and rolling out from under the bed. Then I leapt to my feet and ran like never before.

I heard a startled exclamation behind me as I fled through the door and into the great outdoors. I made for the weeds and brambles as fast as I could, risking only one glance behind me. That one glance was enough to make me want to faint. Roscoe

Thompson was standing outside, rifle against his shoulder, aiming straight for me.

I bit back a scream and ducked below the nearest car as the window shattered above my head. I scrambled behind the next car, and I did scream when another window was shot out from above me. I could hear Roscoe's raging shouts of "Thief! Get back here!" I ducked behind one more car as he began screaming curses.

I took a deep breath and plunged into the weeds, crashing toward freedom. I ran out of the weeds and onto the road, running toward the safety of the gray truck parked in an empty parking lot ahead. I ripped the door open, all but threw myself inside, slammed it behind me, and shrieked, "Drive!"

Luke took one look at me, stomped on the gas, and spun out onto the road. "Are you okay?" he asked worriedly.

"Oh . . . oh, dear," was all I could manage.

The tires on Luke's truck squealed as he whipped onto a tiny deserted road, pulled over, and slammed the truck into park. "Are you hurt?" he demanded.

I took a deep breath and regained my composure with a great deal of effort. "No. I'm fine."

Luke raised an eyebrow. He didn't seem convinced.

"Really I am," I protested weakly. Looking into his concerned eyes, I felt my pent-up fear release in a flood. I moved closer and threw my arms around him, clinging to him as if I feared someone would tear him away. "Oh, Luke," I gasped. "He was shooting at me."

"What?"

"I got out of there, he followed me, and tried to shoot me. I ducked behind the cars, and he shot out two windows."

"Dear Lord," Luke gasped as he held me tighter. "This has to end, Tricia."

"No," I fought back. "We had a deal, remember?"

"It's not worth adding to the death toll!" Luke shot back.

I let my arms slide from his back and sat up rigidly. "Oh, but isn't it worth a life, Luke? It's worth Paul's life! It's worth Aaron's life! The cops are concentrating on Aaron. If we don't find Paul's killer, no one will. Justice will fail. And if the cops find enough trashy evidence, Aaron could spend the majority of his life in prison for a crime he didn't commit! It's worth any price, Luke."

"But this is serious, Tricia!" He grabbed my shoulders and shook me hard. "Roscoe Thompson could have shot you!"

I looked Luke straight in the eye. "But he didn't, did he!"

This time it was Luke who threw his arms about my shoulders and held me tight. "Don't you scare me like that, Tricia Lakely, you hear?"

"All right," I gave in. "From here on out we're more careful, and we call in backup if we need it." We held each other in silence for a few moments before Luke finally released me. "So what did you find out?"

"Roscoe Thompson is really a loan shark."

Luke looked a bit surprised. "So the rumors are true after all?"

"Apparently so. Paul did have a file. His background sheet said that he was paying off his dead mother's medical bills. He's already paid back the original loan and was working on interest. He still owed a few thousand dollars, but I don't know why Roscoe would murder him over that. There was nothing to indicate that Paul wasn't planning to pay it all back over time."

Luke sighed, seemingly disgusted with himself. "So this whole thing, gunshots and all, was a waste?"

"Not exactly," I disagreed. "I don't know if it's important, but Bobby Joe Fink has a loan out too."

"Bobby Joe, the janitor?"

I nodded.

Luke shrugged. "In this game, everything's important."

"I want to know more about our distinguished janitor," I remarked absently.

"I hope you're not suggesting that we go through *his* house now," Luke replied nervously.

"No," I said quickly. "Not yet, anyway. But I do wish I knew if our old friend Sam's got anything on him." I shook my head. "But what I want even more is to know who his partner is. This 'Tommy.' It's going to drive me crazy."

Luke gave me an odd look and suddenly burst out laughing.

"What?" I asked, no idea what on earth could possibly be funny.

"It's so obvious!" he laughed. "It's been in front of our faces the whole time, and we never saw it!"

"What?" I demanded impatiently.

"Who would Tommy be? I mean, think about it. Who's a cop

that you know?"

"I don't know any cops, Luke!" I protested.

He grinned. "But you know their daughters."

"Aauugh!" I buried my face in my hands. "Melissa's dad! How could I miss that?"

Luke couldn't stop laughing. "You're slipping, Tricia."

"Shut up!" I shot back, and then I erupted into helpless laughter as he shook his head, shifted his truck into gear, and pulled back onto the road.

Luke pulled into my driveway and turned off his truck. "I'll just be a few minutes," I promised, as I opened the door and jumped out. I walked up to the front door, pulled it open, and stepped inside. There with their backs to me were my mother and Francis Whitman. Both were seated on the couch. Now where had I seen this before? No, it wasn't déjà vu—this was familiar for a reason. I had seen much the same thing when I walked in the house just yesterday.

"Hi, Mom."

"Oh, hi, honey," she replied, standing up. She walked over. "How was your day?"

"Okay I guess." Mom was a little bit dressed up. Not much, but she wasn't her usual, totally casual self. Communication had always been pretty open between us—especially since Dad died—and she had commented yesterday evening that she thought Francis was nice and all. I guessed that she liked him.

"Hi, Tricia," Francis called from his seat on the couch.

"I've invited Frank over for dinner this evening."

I raised an eyebrow. "Frank?" I mouthed, my back to the couch.

She shrugged. "Frank, Francis," she mouthed back.

"Sorry I'm going to miss it," I said. "I have to go to Paul's funeral, remember?"

"Oh," Mom said, slowly. "I'd forgotten."

Yeah, right. Mom had impeccable timing and an even better memory. Almost everything she did was part of some grand design or another, most of which I would never be able to fig-ure out. At any rate, I knew that she had remembered that I was going to be gone, and she had been planning a nice quiet din-ner for herself and Francis—or Frank—or whatever.

"Well, you guys have fun," I said. "I've got to go change."

"Are you driving yourself?" Mom asked.

"No. I'm riding with Luke."

"Is he coming to pick you up?"

"He's waiting in the driveway." By that time I'd almost made it to my room.

"Why'd you leave him outside? You should have invited him in! I'm going to ask him inside."

I retreated to my bedroom. There was no escape for Luke now. She was going to drag him inside and go through the twenty-questions routine. If Luke Benson had even considered having any interest in me other than friendship, his mind would be changed by the time Mom was through with him.

I pulled my nice black dress out of the back of the closet. It was one of those delightful things that makes the wearer appear much thinner than she really is—a very helpful illusion. I laid it out on my bed and reluctantly retrieved a pair of black heels from my closet. If there's one thing that will do a number on a girl's foot, it's a nasty pair of high heels. Sure, they look nice, but sometimes I have to wonder if it's worth it. I headed across the hall to the bathroom.

I could hear Mom's voice coming from the living room. That probably meant that Luke hadn't run for cover yet. Maybe it wasn't quite as bad as I suspected it would be.

I washed my face and hands, making sure that my nice little romp through the weeds hadn't left any aftereffects. I walked back across to my bedroom, put on the dress and shoes, and then crossed back to the bathroom. Luke was probably wondering what was taking me so long—we had stopped at his house first and he had changed and made it back out to the truck in record time.

I pulled my hair out of the bun. Being twisted into a bun had left a pleasing curl in my hair that luckily didn't brush out. I stared into the mirror for a moment, wondering why people dressed up for funerals. I knew that Paul wouldn't care, and Luke probably wouldn't even notice, but it was just something that was done.

I hoped Paul hadn't minded the wait for his funeral; arrangements had been delayed because the coroner had been out of town over the weekend. I smiled. If I knew Paul, not only would he not mind if we didn't dress up for his funeral, but he probably wouldn't care if none of this fuss was made at all. He would have told the neighbors who paid for his funeral that it was a waste of good money, but I, like the others, thought he was worth a little bit of a fuss.

I flipped off the lights and made my way up the hall. Luke was on the couch with Mom on one side and Francis on the other. "Are you ready, Luke?" I asked.

Luke stood up. "Yes," he replied as he turned around.

"Well, it was nice seeing you again, Luke," Francis said, extending a hand as if they had been discussing a business deal.

Luke shook it. "You too, Mr. Whitman," he replied.

"Drive safely," Mom instructed.

"Yes, ma'am." I gave her a hug. "Bye. You guys have a nice dinner."

"Bye, honey," Mom replied as Luke and I headed for the door.

I stepped outside, shutting the door behind us. "So, how bad was it?" I asked Luke as we headed for the truck.

"What?"

"The before-you-drive-my-daughter-anywhere quiz."

"Oh it wasn't that bad. We just had a conversation."

"You mean she didn't give you some kind of IQ test or anything like that?"

"Nope."

"Luke?"

"Yeah?"

"Where are you going? The driver sits on the other side."

"I know that," he laughed. "Just being polite." With that he pulled open my door and extended a hand.

"Why thank you, sir," I replied graciously. I placed my hand in his and stepped into the truck. He shut the door behind me and walked around the front of the truck to his side as I fastened my seat belt. He opened his own door and got in. "So what's with Mr. Fake British Accent?"

"I think Mom's got a crush on him."

"Oh," Luke replied as he backed out of the driveway and onto the street. "What do you think about him?"

"Oh, I don't know," I replied. "Haven't really made up my mind yet. It's kind of weird, though. Mom hasn't really had any boyfriends since Dad died. I guess it really is time she moved on and dated again, though."

Luke smiled. "Well, I guess there's hope as long as he didn't automatically strike you as a creep."

I shrugged. "Hey, anything's possible. He might be perfect for Mom, for all I know."

"Hi. Rachael? This is Tricia."

"Hey, girl. What's up?"

"Just wanted to talk a bit."

"I know what you mean. I miss Homecoming, you know. It kinda stinks being buried in classes again, and back to taping Burton's stupid lectures. Today's was quite stirring, wouldn't you say?"

"Yeah, right. How can you stand to listen to that twice? Doesn't it give you a headache?"

"I'm surprised it doesn't give *him* a headache. Still, I only tape the big quiz or test reviews to help me study."

"I'll bet you have about a million of those little miniature tapes scattered all over your room just waiting to torture you with another episode of Burton's cracking voice."

"I do seem to run out of tapes every time I turn around. I always keep the quiz ones for the test, and I never seem to have enough old ones to record over. Still, it's all worth it. If I don't make a real good grade in there, Dad's not going to let me try out for volleyball this year. It's like he wants me to be class valedictorian or something. It's really annoying, you know. When's the last time you got chewed out for making a B on a history test?"

"You're not serious!"

"Close enough. Hey, I told you. He wants me to go off to Stanford and be a brain surgeon or something. I don't know. Anyway, you'll never guess what happened to me this afternoon."

"What?"

"Your new neighbor, you know, the cute guy? He was stopped on the side of the road when I was coming home from school. Well, it turned out that he had run out of gas. Oops! So, anyway, he gave me a gas can from his trunk and I went and got some for him. He was going to take his trash to the Dumpsters or something. I even took his trash for him. Wasn't that neighborly?"

"Yeah. I think he was talking about something like that when I came home tonight."

"That one flew right by me. When did you see him tonight?"

"Oh, he and Mom had dinner while I was at Paul's funeral. She's got a little crush on him."

"Oh. Can't blame her there—he *is* good lookin'. But I'll tell you one thing, that man has lousy trash bags. The darn thing broke on me when I was getting it out of the trunk. Luckily there wasn't anything gross in it. Mostly boxes and stuff. Probably from unpacking. Anyway I finally got it all picked up and got his gas for him. So that's my spiel for the day. Now it's your turn. What's on your mind?"

"A lot of stuff. I went to Paul's funeral this evening. It was really nice and all, except that there weren't many people there. His parents are dead, and he was an only child. He had a few aunts and uncles and cousins. Grandma Harriet called them, but they all live on the west coast, and they couldn't make it out to the funeral. It's kind of sad that none of his family came. All of his neighbors came, though. Everybody loved Paul. The street just won't be the same without him."

"Yeah," Rachael said sympathetically. "Things are always hard when people die."

"They're not usually this hard, though. This has affected all of Judsonville. And school! Man, you'd think Aaron had some kind of deadly, contagious disease or something."

"Yeah. Everybody says you and Luke Benson have been hanging out with him and Joe Taylor lately. What's up with that?"

"Aaron just needed a friend."

"Yeah, I guess so. Nearly the whole school thinks he did it, what with the knife and the penalty and all. Especially since the cops are coming down hard on him and everything. His is the only name that's come up in connection with the murder so far, so they don't have anyone else to suspect. Rumors fly like wildfire."

"What do you think?" I asked.

"I don't know. There's no way to know for sure, but somehow I can't see Aaron Tyler killing someone in cold blood."

"Neither can I."

"Some people say that you guys are up to something. Nobody seems to know what, but some people say you're trying to cover Aaron up."

"Yeah, right," I snorted. "There's nothing to cover up. If the cops have the knife, what do they think we can change?"

"I don't know."

"They've been watching too much 'Matlock.'"

"Tell me about it."

"They are right about one thing, though."

"What's that?"

"We *are* up to something."

"Oh, dear. Don't tell me. You're really employed by the CIA and you're engaged in top secret espionage."

"Close. But not quite."

"How close?" she asked, startled.

"Well, the CIA isn't involved, but from a certain point of view, you might include espionage. . . . Although, I'd call it just ordinary everyday snooping."

"Tricia the spy? Yeah, right! You'd better start explaining."

"Well, this isn't top secret, but it definitely ain't common knowledge. You're gonna have to keep this to yourself, okay?"

"No prob." Rachael was entering "intrigue" mode. Scheming and secrets were her cup of tea.

"Okay, the long and short of it is that I know for a fact that Aaron Tyler didn't kill Paul Sanders. Aaron, Joe, Luke, and I are going to prove it by uncovering the real killer."

"You're not serious," she said skeptically.

"Serious as a heart attack. But I need your help."

"More espionage?" Rachael asked hopefully.

"Sort of, but not quite."

"Shucks. What do you need me to do?"

"First I need to ask you a question. Is doing something behind a friend's back the same as being dishonest with her, if it's for a good cause, and it's not going to hurt her in any way?"

"Just out of curiosity, does this apply to me?"

"No. Melissa Hall."

"What's going on, and what does this have to do with me helping you?"

"I need you to help me do something without Melissa knowing it. You gotta trust me on this one, Rachael."

"Oh, I trust you, Tricia. You're my best friend, and if I didn't trust you, I'd have hung up on you by now."

"Okay. Ya ready for this?"

"Can't wait. Explain away."

"Well—it goes like this. . . ."

CHAPTER SEVEN

Rachael fit into a conspiracy like Cinderella's foot slid into the glass slipper. I had to admire her. That little blonde had twisted the conversation around just right to get Melissa to invite us to a sleepover, without even realizing that she was being manipulated. I really hated to sneak around behind Melissa's back like this, but one doesn't just tell a friend that one wants to spy on her dad. How was I supposed to explain that it wasn't that I didn't trust her dad? It was Sam that was the problem. I didn't know whether to trust Tommy Hall or not.

Melissa had made the offhand comment that her dad got a phone call from his partner around seven every night, and Rachael's little tape recorder was nestled in my overnight bag, waiting to record that conversation. So the basic plan was for Rachael (my new partner in crime) and me to sit around and wait for seven o'clock to come and try not to feel too guilty.

"Why don't we go to the game?" Melissa suggested.

I wondered how many people would actually show up for this game. It might be against a tough team, but last week's murder had probably scared off a few of the less fanatical fans. It was strange to think that all of this had begun but a week ago—it felt like at least a month.

"Are you sure that's a good idea, Melissa?" Rachael asked, probably searching for an excuse not to go. After all, football games started at seven and it was hard to tape record a phone conversation if one was at a football stadium instead.

"Come on, Rachael!" Melissa protested. "That was just a freak incident. We all enjoy football games, and we shouldn't let one random murder stop us from going."

"Well, let's not go just yet," I suggested. "Let's wait a bit. I wanted to ask you guys something, and the game will still be there. It won't make a big difference if we're a few minutes late, you know." I glanced at my watch. Quarter to seven. I was going to have to stall for fifteen minutes, and then came the problem of getting rid of Melissa so I could record the message.

"What do you want to know?" Melissa asked curiously.

One thing at a time. . . . "I wanted to ask your opinion on something," I began slowly.

"What?" Melissa prompted.

"Well," I said, trying not to look embarrassed. "What do you guys think about Luke Benson?!"

"Luke Benson?" they exclaimed in unison. I sighed.

"Are you about ready to go, Tricia?" Melissa asked as the phone rang.

"Yes," I replied tensely.

She stepped calmly into the room, picked up her phone, and said, "Hello? . . . Just a minute."

She hurried out of the room and called, "Daddy! It's for you!" Then she turned back to me. "I'm going to go start up the car and get it warmed up."

"All right," I agreed.

"Oh, Tricia?"

"Yes?"

"Would you hang up that phone for me?"

"Sure." I let out a deep breath as Melissa disappeared. Luck was certainly on my side tonight. I moved for my bag, jerked out the little tape recorder, hit RECORD, and placed it next to the phone. I looked up as Rachael slipped back into the room. "Keep watch, would you?" I whispered. She nodded and headed out the door.

I nervously waited, barely hearing the voices leaking from the phone. I could also hear a very welcome sound outside. It was the coughing of an engine that just wasn't starting. I tensed as the sound ceased, and a few minutes later, Melissa appeared in the doorway. "I've left my lights on, and the battery's dead," Melissa said. "Could you give me a jump, Tricia?"

"Of course," I replied, heading for the door before Melissa could step inside and hear the faint voices or the buzz of the tape recorder. "Watch it for me," I mouthed back over my shoulder. Rachael nodded.

It took about five minutes to charge up Melissa's car, and by the time we made it back inside, the phone was safely back on the hook and Rachael was tying her shoelaces.

"Ready?" Melissa asked.

Rachael nodded, and we headed for the door.

"Bye, Mom!" Melissa called.

The words "Be careful!" rang after us as we stepped through the door.

We climbed into Melissa's car and headed for the football game.

As I circled the track around the football field, I saw Luke watching me from the stands, Steve Johnson throwing passes and scoring touchdowns, and Joe Taylor recovering the Hornets' fumbles left and right. I found Aaron seated alone on the bench looking utterly lost.

My heart went out to him, and once more the unfairness of it all struck a deafening blow. At that particular moment I was a bit upset with Coach Jones. After all, it was Aaron's senior year. I sighed. Sometimes I guess life just stinks and there's nothing you can do about it.

I headed up the steps of the student section and wordlessly sat down beside Luke. His friends were all there, and so were a lot of other people from school, but he didn't seem to mind. I looked at him carefully, realizing that he didn't even seem uncomfortable with my presence. He must have known what everyone was thinking. But he didn't say a word. He just sat there.

I felt his hand reach for mine, and for once I ignored the screaming logic that urged me to pull away. Instead I trusted my emotions and closed my hand around his. He turned his head and smiled at me.

I was never quite sure why football games made me so restless—by halftime, I just couldn't stand to sit still anymore. I reluctantly let go of Luke's warm hand and stood up. Leaving him with a reassuring smile, I turned and descended the stairs.

As I jumped off the bottom step and onto the track, I nearly walked right into Francis Whitman. "Hello, Tricia!"

"Hi," I replied awkwardly.

"How's your mom?"

"Just fine," I answered, putting on one of those automatic and half-fake smiles.

"That's good," he smiled.

"Well, see you around," I said, quickly heading away from him. I really didn't want to get into an hour-long conversation with my mom's boyfriend. I barely knew him. I sighed as I spotted a figure leaning against the fence on the other side of the field. I wondered how Sam Buckson was analyzing the situation. I guessed that his view and mine were worlds apart.

Spotting Bobby Joe Fink, who was heading for the field house, I followed him, deciding to find out what he was up to. He was headed for the side door, so I darted around the field house, took a quick glance to either side to make sure no one was about to see me, pulled open the back door, and jumped inside. I could hear the side door opening as Bobby Joe stepped inside.

I found myself, once again, standing out in the open because I had failed to think things through before I rushed into a situation. Luke was slowly corrupting me with male thinking. I took one look at the door standing ajar directly across the hall, and darted through it. I found myself in a room with a huge cabinet across the side wall, a tiny counter in the corner, and a big whirlpool directly in the center. This could be a motivation to join the football team—the guys got to play with the whirlpool. Of course it was probably for sore muscles or something to that effect, but still. . . . At any rate, the thing at least provided a place to hide.

Bobby Joe strolled straight past the whirlpool room and headed into the room beside it. The sound of a flushing toilet next door quickly identified it as the bathroom. I climbed out of the whirlpool, tiptoed out of the room, took a right, and headed to the main room of the field house. I took a quick look at the lay of the land. I needed to remember every little detail—I was in unfamiliar territory here.

I heard footsteps down the hall and figured that I had better find a hiding place within the next two seconds if I wanted to be out of sight before Bobby Joe appeared. I took one look at the couch in the corner, climbed over the back, and slid behind it. One second later, right on cue, he clomped into the room.

Crouching low in the tiny corner, my knees pressed against my chest, I peered through the tiny gap between the back corner of the couch and the wall. Bobby Joe idly wandered about the room, glancing at the items hanging on the hooks or lying on the high shelves of the open lockers.

He absently picked up the gold pocket watch lying on top of the neatly folded stack of clothes atop the shelf of one locker.

The watch, with an exquisite carving of a tree on the front, belonged to Steve Johnson. It had belonged to his grandfather, who had given it to him on his deathbed. Steve carried that watch with him everywhere. I held back the gasp that threatened to escape as Bobby Joe held the watch up by its gold chain and looked at it almost speculatively.

Why that no good . . . if he even thought about taking Steve's watch. . . . Bobby Joe closed his hand about the watch and moved his hand toward his pocket. His hand froze rigidly just above the pocket and then moved away again. He opened his hand, gazed at the watch, sighed, and replaced it atop Steve's clothing. I resisted the urge to sigh as well—a sigh of relief.

It would have been so easy for him to put that watch in his pocket and walk away. If that was the case, then what was to stop him from taking Aaron's pocketknife? And if he was desperate enough for money to steal a watch that meant the world to the guy who owned it, then what was to stop him from killing some guy he didn't even know for a handsome profit? The whole prospect was more than a little disturbing.

I held my breath and ducked away from the gap as Bobby Joe turned around and headed straight for me. I cringed as he plopped onto the couch and it inched slightly backward. He was motionless for a few moments, and then the couch began to shudder. I gently placed my hand against the back of it, wondering what on earth was going on.

Then a surprising sound shed the light of realization upon me. He was crying! I could hear his soft whimpers as the couch quivered with his shaking.

A twisting pity crept into my heart, but with it came an uncomfortable reality. Bobby Joe Fink was obviously upset, and who was to say that it wasn't because he had killed an innocent man?

But then, who was to say that it was? Maybe he was just weary of his financial situation. My heart went out to him, but my will kept it restrained. If he was Paul's killer, then there was no compassion within me for him. If there was one thing I knew, it was that I could never have even a drop of sympathy for a murderer.

Bobby Joe didn't cry for long, but he stayed on the couch for about five more minutes before he slowly stood up and walked resolutely away. I waited tensely for the sound of the door closing behind him. When it came, I gratefully stood up, my cramped knees threatening to buckle. I climbed back over the couch and stood in the middle of the room, shifting from foot to foot, waiting for feeling to come back into my feet. I gazed at the row of open lockers along the walls. Above each wooden frame, a number was painted in blue on the white wall.

As my eyes fell on the last locker, the blue number standing proudly above it, I smiled and moved toward it. I gazed up at the perfectly rounded curves of the painted number *99*, and then my eyes moved to the nameplate affixed to the top frame of the locker: AARON TYLER. I ran my finger across the tiny engraved metal plate slowly.

"No matter what," I whispered into the locker, "I'll set things right. Don't worry, Aaron."

I sighed, turned away, and headed back down the hall toward the back door. The last thing I needed was to get caught snooping around the field house. I have no idea how I would have explained that one.

CHAPTER EIGHT

The anticipation was about to kill me. I didn't have to drag Luke inside this time—he was as impatient as I was. Mom and Francis were sitting together at the table again, and I offered only the briefest of greetings before Luke and I retreated to my room. I pulled out the tape recorder, my hand nearly shaking with excitement. Luke and I looked at each other, and a faint smile flickered across his mouth. I took a deep breath and hit the PLAY button on Rachael's borrowed tape recorder.

"Yeah, Mary and the kids are doing fine." The voice belonged to Tommy Hall, Melissa's dad.

"Good, good." There was our old buddy Sam Buckson. I smiled. "You know, Tommy," Sam continued, "I want to check in with Henry again and see how things are going down there. Thursday's kind of a light day for the boys, so I think the other coaches can handle things if I pull Henry out for a few minutes."

"Yeah," Tommy agreed.

"And I think you should stop in with Nancy Tate and make sure everything's all right down at the school."

"Yeah," Tommy replied. I could tell who the brains in this operation was.

"I think we should also talk to Harriet Lakely again, too." I sighed. Poor Grandma. She was traumatized enough already. "We can go ahead and do that on Monday," Sam continued. "And then on Tuesday we'll run down to the school, and while you chat with Nancy Tate, I'll check and see if they've gotten any tips in the box."

Fat chance, Sam, I thought. They had put out a box where anyone at Carrier High could submit an anonymous tip, but we all knew that it wasn't going to happen. I doubted that any of the students knew anything, and if they did, they wouldn't be stupid enough to dump a note in that box. The tip wouldn't be anonymous if the killer knew who had given it.

"Sometime I want to give Paul's house one final run-through.

In the meantime, I want you and the boys working on that '286AHD'. We came up empty on a license plate check. I'll buy a week's supply of doughnuts for the man who figures it out. Heck, I'll buy doughnuts for the whole department. But I want an answer, and as soon as possible, Tommy. Help me out here, please."

"Yeah." I was starting to wonder if the man had a one-word vocabulary.

"Well, that's about it. I'll see you on Monday, Tommy. Hope you wake up chock-full of ideas, because I'm running out."

"I'll see what I can do, Sam," Tommy promised. It was good to know that he could speak after all. "See you Monday then."

"Monday," Sam confirmed.

There was a tiny click and then another louder click as the background noise faded off the tape. I punched the STOP button. That was it. I looked up at Luke.

"Sure would be nice if we knew what '286AHD' meant," he said. "From what we know, we're probably already ahead of the cops, and if we knew what that number was, it would give us a permanent edge. It's got to be important."

I sighed. "I have no idea. The number's just going to have to wait for now. I think we need to check in with Coach Jones too."

Luke nodded. "Yeah. We never thought much about him."

"Well that's because . . . you know. . . ," I stuttered.

"He's not exactly the kind of guy who would come to mind as a murder suspect," Luke finished for me.

"Right," I said. "That's it. I mean, we've all respected him our whole life. It's not easy to even consider that he could be capable of something like this."

"But it's possible, you know," Luke replied.

"I know," I sighed. "But it's still weird."

"What *hasn't* been weird so far?" Luke smiled. "You know, Tricia," Luke said with a wink, "by the time we're done with this, we're going to be such experts that the CIA is going to be down on its knees begging us to work for them."

I winked back. "Keep dreaming, dear."

Jackie looked a bit unsure. I wondered how she was taking all of this as Luke and I walked up to the spot where she and Aaron always sat together before school. "Could I talk to you for a minute, Aaron?"

Aaron glanced at Jackie, looked back up at me, and replied, "Sure." He stood up. "I'll be back in a sec, Jackie."

As Aaron and I headed for the stairwell, I glanced over my shoulder and saw Luke already talking to Jackie. I smiled. It was nice to have someone I could count on. I stopped at the corner and turned to face Aaron, careful to stay in Jackie's sight. The last thing I needed was for her to start worrying about her boyfriend's faithfulness.

"How's Jackie taking all this, Aaron?"

He shrugged. "She's just kind of confused. She knows that I didn't do it, but she doesn't understand all the snubbing and the suspicious looks. She's trying to deal with it."

"What does she know?" I asked.

"She doesn't know anything about what you and Luke are doing. As far as I know only you, Luke, Joe, and I know about that. I didn't tell Jackie because I didn't want to complicate things for her even more. She's worried enough as it is. I wish I could tell her that everything's going to be all right."

"It will, Aaron," I promised.

Aaron shook his head. "Why do you care about me so much, Tricia? Why are you here for me when everyone but Jackie and Joe is gone?"

I smiled. "Because once upon a time you were there for me, remember?"

"But that was last year. And I didn't do anything all that special."

I shook my head in disagreement. "It was special to me. I was still struggling with my dad's death, and listening was what I needed. You were a friend when I needed one the most." I smiled at him. "I need to talk to you and Joe at lunch while Jackie's eating in the hall with her friends."

Aaron nodded and moved back across the hall to Jackie. Luke and I headed down the hall, ready to face our morning classes.

"Let me guess," Joe said with a grin. "You need us to do your dirty work for you again."

"Nah," I replied. "Just need you to cover it up."

Joe sighed. "How come you get to do all the fun stuff? What if Aaron and I wanted to be the spies?"

"Well, there are people watching every move Aaron makes.

In fact, one might say the same about you."

"Not sure I follow," Joe admitted.

"You know," I replied. "Aaron—magnetic cops. . . ."

"Yeah," Joe replied slowly. "But nobody's watching me."

"Really?" I asked with a raised eyebrow. I nodded toward my normal circle a few tables to the right. "Then what do you call that?"

Joe glanced over at the table and quickly turned back to me. He seemed a bit surprised.

"And what do you see, Joe?"

"Girls," he replied uncomfortably.

"And I'll bet not one of their eyes was even wandering in your direction. . . ."

"All right, all right," Joe gave in. "I bow to your supreme spying power and awesome intellect."

I grinned. "And I submit to your superior good looks."

"Whatever," he laughed. "So how can we be of service to you, my dear?" he asked gallantly.

"I need you to help us get into the field house on Thursday."

"Why?" Aaron asked.

"Sam Buckson's going to talk to Coach Jones, and I want to know what's said."

"You're going to spy on the coach?" Joe asked incredulously.

I shrugged. "Sure. Why not?"

"You don't actually think he did it?" Aaron asked cautiously.

"No," I admitted. "But he might have some useful information. At any rate, I need you two to get Luke and me into the field house without being seen by any of the other guys, and cover for us while we spy. Can you swing that?"

Aaron looked at Joe uncertainly. Joe broke out into a grin. "Sounds like fun to me!"

Aaron shook his head. "We're going to be accomplices to a pair of spies."

Joe shrugged. "Almost as good as being spies ourselves. We get to share the excitement."

"Don't forget the danger," I warned.

Joe grinned. "Danger? I laugh in the face of danger!"

I could almost hear the theme music from *Mission Impossible* playing in my head as Luke and I crouched against the block wall, staring at the field house barely ten feet away. The concrete stands on the away side were nestled up against a tall, rocky hill, and there wasn't much room for us to hide behind them. But it was a perfect place for Luke and me to watch the field house without being seen ourselves.

One glance at Luke's face revealed his tenseness. I reached behind me, and the moment my hand closed around his, some of the rigidness worked its way out of the fingers that tightened around mine. I understood why almost all of the movie heroes had a partner or someone to keep them courageous and strong during their adventures. Heck, even Superman needed Lois Lane.

Luke gave my hand a squeeze as a welcome sound came to our ears. There was no mistaking the sound of dozens of guys tromping out the front door of a field house and stampeding onto a field. We crouched frozen behind the bleachers until all the sound effects were coming from the field, not the field house.

Just then, the back door of the field house flew open and Joe's head popped out. Luke and I edged to the corner of the bleachers, peering at the players on the field. The guys had moved to the center of the field, and we could see only a few of them. Everyone's attention seemed focused elsewhere, so Luke and I sprinted across that dangerous ten feet or so of empty space, still hand in hand.

Safely behind the field house, we made for the back steps. "Got it to yourselves," Joe said quickly. "They're all outside." And with that he was gone, heading for the front door. Luke motioned me in ahead of him, and we stepped inside.

"We have to find the coach's office," Luke said. "What's that way?" He pointed to the left.

"The main room," I replied. "And across the hall is the whirlpool."

Luke nodded. We took a right down the hallway. We passed a door on the left which I remembered was the bathroom, then slipped through the door at the end of the hall, where we found ourselves standing in an office. It seemed like a couple thousand people had been through this place, and each one had left something behind him. There were all kinds of odds and ends, a copier in the corner, and about a million and two papers scattered about the office, a telltale sign that it was used by several people.

Two doors opened from the office—one was the side door to

the outside. Further investigation proved that the other led to our destination. This small room in the very back corner of the field house was, indeed, Coach Jones's office.

"Now what?" Luke asked. "We don't seem to have many options for hiding places in here."

I nodded. "I know." My eyes scanned the room quickly, searching for anything promising. The room held a desk, a filing cabinet, a table with three huge boxes lying under it, a single potted plant in a corner, and a few chairs. The pictures on the wall of past football teams and of the crowd running onto the field after last year's championship game gave the place a homey sort of atmosphere that could have made any football player or fan feel right at home.

The first place I checked was the desk. Maybe hiding under desks was the oldest trick in the book, but my only education in spying had come from the stereotypes in the movies. Unfortunately, the drawers weren't going to leave enough room for both me and Coach Jones's feet. Besides, he'd be able to see me easily. The potted plant was too small to be any help at all. Since Luke and I certainly weren't going to fit in a filing cabinet, that left the table.

I moved to the table, which was sandwiched in the corner between the wall and the filing cabinet. I dropped to my knees and pulled out one of the boxes. I had no idea what was in it, but it felt like a ton of bricks. Since it was taped shut, I wasn't going to snoop. I stared at the boxes for a moment. They weren't pushed back against the wall, but in rather easy reach. I sighed.

"Let me guess," Luke said dryly.

I shrugged. "At least it's not a bed."

"No," he agreed. He got down on his knees and crawled through the space and under the table. I crawled under after him and pulled the heavy box back into place. As the dark closed in, I could almost feel a ridiculously huge comforter pressing against me. . . .

The floor was cold and hard, and after a few long moments of staring at the underside of the wooden table, fear began to seep in. And then Luke's hand was there, closing around mine. I looked over at him, and I could make out his reassuring smile. For one irrational moment, I wanted nothing more than to lean over and kiss him on the spot.

I might have, but at that very moment, the office door opened and two pairs of feet passed by the little crack of light I peered through. I could see Coach Jones sit down in the chair behind his desk. The other man sat down in another chair in front of the desk, and even though his back was to me, I knew it was Sam Buckson.

"So how have you been doing, Sam?" Coach Jones asked.

"Fine, fine."

"What brings you over to see me today?"

"Well, I wanted to check in and see how things have been going."

"What sort of things?"

"You know, Henry. How the team's doing, if there's been any strange behavior, how Aaron's doing, and so forth."

"Well, the team's as well as can be expected," Coach Jones replied. "And as for Aaron, I had no choice but to bench him for the time-being. It's not fair to him, but suspicions are flying every which way. Until you fix this mess, I can't let him play without complaints that stop just short of open accusations."

Sam shook his head. "I'm sorry about Aaron, but there's no help for it. There's nothing to prove he's not the man I'm looking for."

"Suspicions and rumors spread like crazy in a little town like this," Coach Jones sighed.

"Well, if everyone knew what I know, you wouldn't be anywhere near free of suspicion yourself, Henry."

"What do you mean?"

"Come on, Henry. Everyone's suspicions about Aaron are based on the fact that there were scouts out to see him at that game, and he screwed up. What they don't know is that there were people watching for you, too. The fact that your team lost wouldn't reflect well on you, either. What's to stop them from thinking that maybe it was you who killed that ref?"

Coach Jones shrugged. "But they don't know, do they? And they won't know about those scouts unless the time comes that I have to resign to go coach at college level."

My thoughts were racing. The clipping on Paul's bulletin board. . . . He had said that he thought the high school coaches had a chance at this one. What if he was right. . . . And continuing with the what-ifs, what if there was something to what Sam Buckson had just said. The very thought that Coach Jones could do anything like that was almost inconceivable. Almost.

"I won't have any new suspicions dragging this school, this team, or me through the dirt," Coach Jones continued.

"Look, Henry," Sam said, "we've known each other all our lives. I don't want this brought up again—not by you, me, or anyone else. Right now the public's focus is on Aaron. Until I gather enough information to decide whether or not to arrest him, I don't need any more pressure from the public. I want you to stay out of this and keep that reputation all shiny, Henry. Are we agreed?"

"Agreed."

"Do you think that Aaron Tyler is capable of murder?"

Coach Jones shrugged. "That's a tough question, Sam."

"I mean, is he *physically* capable of murder?"

"You mean could he walk up and knife that man, even if it meant a little bit of wrestling?"

"That's what I mean."

"Well, then, yes. He's a strong boy. Well, heck, Sam. Just about anybody could knife a man if he wanted to bad enough."

"We know that Aaron Tyler could have killed Paul Sanders. How about that tough question, then, Henry? Do you think Aaron *would* commit murder?"

Coach Jones shook his head. "I honestly don't know, Sam."

"Do you know about his father?"

"Yes."

"Do you think there could be some sort of connection between the two?"

Coach Jones shook his head. "That boy is not his father."

"Well, Henry, why don't you help me out by keeping your mouth shut about coaching scouts and your eyes open for strange behavior from your boys. Let me know if anything happens that I should know about."

Coach Jones nodded. "All right, Sam. I'll keep you posted."

I could feel the scrape of the chair against the floor as Sam scooted it back and stood up. "Thank you Henry. I'll be seeing you." With that, he turned and headed for the door.

His footsteps paused for a moment, and I heard Coach Jones's voice say, "Sam?"

"Yes?"

"Would you tell one of the coaches to send in Joe Taylor?"

My hand tightened on Luke's.

CHAPTER NINE

The familiar form of Joe Taylor appeared in my tiny crack of light a few moments later. "Yes, Coach?" he asked as he stood in front of the desk.

"Have a seat, son." Joe sat down, and Coach Jones continued. "What have you been up to lately, son?"

"What?" Joe asked, surprised.

"What have you and Aaron been up to lately?"

"What do you mean, Coach?"

"Now you don't honestly expect me to believe that you and Aaron are taking all of this sitting down, do you, Joe? I know the both of you better than that. So, Joseph, I ask again: what have you and Aaron been up to?"

Joe shrugged. "What could Aaron or I do to change the fact that he's a prime suspect in a murder that he didn't commit?"

"You tell me, son. That's what I'm asking you."

"We can't change what the cops think, and we can't change the fact that someone took Aaron's knife from the field house. We can't change the shallow suspicious stares that get thrown in our direction from half the people in this narrow-minded school, and we can't even change the fact that the real killer's probably sitting on his butt watching TV right now. All we can do this time is stick together and deal with it."

Coach Jones gave Joe a long, penetrating gaze. "I don't want you two getting yourselves into any more trouble than you're in already," Coach Jones said. "And no matter what, I want you to promise me right now that you're not going to violate my trust in any way."

"What do you think is going on here, Coach? Why should you have any reason not to trust us?"

"I'm not sure what's going on, Joe. But I want you to keep your nose out of it."

"Coach," Joe said seriously, "you don't actually believe that Aaron's guilty, do you?"

Coach Jones was silent for a long moment. "I don't *want* to believe he is."

"Then why did you bench him? None of this is his fault."

"Son, it wasn't you or me who left a knife lying in the field house or got into an argument with a ref."

"Maybe, but you know it's not fair, Coach. Why do you have to bench him?"

"You know that there'd be fits left and right if I didn't, Joe. When it comes to narrow-minded people in this town, you may just be right. But while I may not want to believe that one of my boys is a murderer, the truth is that I just don't know. But," Coach Jones warned, "I do know that I want you to promise me right now that you'll stay out of mischief. If Aaron gets into trouble, you stay out of it. You just remember that this is Aaron Tyler's fight, not yours—whatever comes of it is between him and God, you hear?"

"That's your opinion, Coach."

"Well you don't have to agree with me, but that's the way I want things to be." Coach Jones sighed. "Go on then, boy."

I wasn't sure how long Luke and I lay there after that. The Coach sat at his desk for a while, and then he left and went back outside again. Luke and I didn't dare move for fear that someone would come back in and catch us at it.

Finally, we could hear a commotion in the main room and we knew that practice was over. For several long minutes there were sounds all over the field house, and then quiet gradually took over as more people left. Someone came in and turned off the lights in the Coach's office. Shortly after that, we heard the door shut, and the whole field house was quiet. A few moments later, the door opened and closed again and there were footsteps in the hall.

A shadowed figure appeared in the office and whispered urgently, "Tricia? Luke?"

It was Joe. "We're here," I answered him.

Joe looked around. "Where?"

"Under the table."

"Okay. I'm going to get out of here before they start to wonder if I got lost. I told Coach I left something. Go out the back and lock the door behind you. Aaron and I'll be waiting by the back gate."

"Okay," I whispered.

With that Joe was gone, jogging back to the front door. After the front door closed again, we waited for a few moments just to make sure that they were gone. Then I gave the box a push and slid it away from the table.

I was surprised at how stiff I was as I rolled over and awkwardly crawled through the hole and into the middle of the office. Luke followed just as clumsily, and I moved the box back behind him. Then both of us somehow managed to stand up.

"Whew," I sighed. "That was odd, wasn't it?"

All Luke could manage was a weak laugh.

On the way to the back door I learned to walk again, and by the time I got there, I had worked the stiffness out of my legs and I wasn't hobbling anymore. I turned the lock and carefully pulled the door open. I gestured for Luke to go ahead, and I turned the lock back again, stepped outside, and closed the door after me.

We slipped silently behind the away stands. From there we darted behind the cheerleading building next to the huge concrete structure. Finally, we were at the back gate, where Aaron and Joe were waiting for us.

"Wait a minute!" I said, staring with dismay at the lock on the gate.

"I'm two jumps ahead of you, Tricia dear," Aaron replied smugly, opening his palm to reveal a silver key. He reached down, unlocked the gate, and pulled it open.

I stared at him incredulously. "Where did you get that?" I demanded.

"Coach Jones dropped it by accident."

"Really?" I wasn't convinced.

"Close enough."

Pizza Hut may not be the greatest place on the planet to have a spy convention, but it worked for us. Actually, there are few better places for a group of teenagers to disappear. We sat in a corner booth, just about the sole occupants of the restaurant.

"What did you find out?" Aaron asked eagerly.

Luke and I exchanged a look. "It seems your coach is keeping some secrets from you guys," he replied.

"Like what?" Joe asked uncomfortably.

"For one thing," I said, "Aaron wasn't the only one who had scouts watching him at that Homecoming game."

"What do you mean?" Aaron asked sharply.

"A college coaching scout was watching the Homecoming game," I continued.

Aaron and Joe looked stunned. "Well, I guess that explains why he was so mad," Aaron managed.

My thoughts went back to that fateful day not so long ago when I had gotten myself into this mess. . . . Steve Johnson had said, "I certainly hope Coach didn't just call us out here to yell some more. He did enough of that last night."

"Why didn't he tell us?" Joe asked.

"He didn't want to say anything unless he knew he had gotten the job," Luke replied.

"I suspect he didn't want to disrupt the season with any news like that," I added.

Aaron's face was losing some of its color. "That gives him a motive," he said quietly. "Tricia, you don't really think—"

"I don't know, Aaron," I sighed. "I certainly hope not."

"Me too," Joe and Aaron agreed in unison.

"At any rate," I continued, "Sam Buckson told him to keep his mouth shut about it because he didn't need any new complications or public suspicions."

"So if he did do it, Buckson's just going to cover for him?" Aaron asked incredulously.

I suspected that he was having a hard enough time even conceiving that Coach Henry Jones was capable of murder, much less that he had cops covering for him. "Yup. He doesn't want reputations dragged through the dirt."

"What about *my* reputation?" Aaron asked disgustedly.

Luke shrugged. "He wasn't *your* high school buddy," he pointed out.

"Yeah," Aaron snorted.

"Coach Jones also wanted me and you to stay out of trouble, Aaron," Joe added.

"What do you mean?"

"Well, he suspects we're into something."

"He knows we're snooping?"

"He suspects something like that."

"Great."

"It's not so bad," Joe disagreed. "We're not actually doing the snooping you know, we're just covering for the snoopers. He doesn't know that Luke and Tricia are in on it, so as long as we're careful, we stay out of trouble. But at school, we're going to have to start being really careful. He said he'd be keeping his eye on us."

Aaron let out a long sigh. "You know what?" he said gloomily. "This really bites."

"Don't you get depressed on me, Aaron Tyler!" I exclaimed.

"Don't I have a right to be?" he shot back. "You're not the one who's a murder suspect here. You should see the suspicious looks that stupid waitress's been giving me!"

"Look, Aaron, sometimes life just sucks—like right now, for example. But we're all going to get through this together. I want us all to make a pact, right here and now," I said slowly. "I want us to promise that we're going to stick together and not give up until this is all resolved. What do you say?"

Aaron thrust his hand to the center of the table. I smiled as Joe's and Luke's hands quickly stacked on his. I closed my hand over Luke's, closed my eyes, and prayed that the truth would be revealed in time.

As we pulled back our hands, I spotted the waitress headed toward our table, pizzas in hand and suspicion written all over her face. Someday soon we were going to prove her wrong— we'd prove them *all* wrong.

"You know, Joe," I said, "you're already breaking your promise to Coach Jones."

"What promise?"

"Remember, he made you promise not to violate his trust by doing anything like this. Which you just swore not to give up."

Joe smiled as he reached for a slice of pepperoni pizza. "But I didn't promise him anything."

"Yes you did. He made you promise—"

"Yes, but he rushed on before I could promise. I can't very well break a promise I never made, can I?"

"No," I grinned. "I guess not."

"Tricia?" Luke asked.

"Hmm?"

"What are we going to do next?"

"Snoop through Bobby Joe's house," I answered promptly.

Aaron's head jerked up. "You're not serious!"

"He's been acting weird, he's got a file at Roscoe Thompson's, plus easy access to the field house. I think that's starting to make him more than a little suspicious. That makes him a new prime suspect in my book."

"All right," Aaron surrendered. "You just be careful!"

I smiled sweetly. "When am I *not* careful?"

A pair of dim red brake lights glowed from the old truck ahead of us. Then a yellow signal light made a feeble attempt to blink, and the vehicle turned off the roadway. It parked in a space in front of an old and probably run-down apartment building hidden behind the main streets of downtown Judsonville. Luke hit the gas and cruised on past.

As soon as we were out of sight of the building, we pulled into the closest driveway and turned around. Luke crept slowly along with his lights on low as the apartment building came back into view.

Bobby Joe was walking toward one of the doors. The tarnished number *12* faintly reflected back to us as the lights ran across the door. I watched carefully as Bobby Joe bent down and picked something up from under the scrawny bush beside the doorstep.

As we passed back by, I glued my eyes to the rearview mirror. I watched with surprise as Bobby Joe's hands moved across the thing in his hands and a silver key emerged that shone back the reddish color of Luke's taillights. The last thing I saw before a curve took him out of sight was Bobby Joe bending down to replace the whatever-it-was back under the scrawny bush.

I looked at Luke as we drove away. His eyes were fixed on the road, and they looked droopy. Maybe it was only eight o'clock, but I was sure he could use some rest. "Hey Luke?"

"Hmm?" he answered distantly.

"Let me drive."

"What?" he asked quickly. "Why?"

"You're tired. Pull over and let me drive."

"Aw, Tricia."

I knew he loved his truck, but surely he had learned to trust me by now. Besides, I knew an exhausted person when I saw one. "Pull over, Luke."

He must have really been tired, because he didn't argue anymore. Instead he put on his blinker at the next deserted parking lot, pulled over, and put the truck into park.

"Thank you," I said simply as I got out and walked around the truck. Luke slid over and buckled his seat belt as I climbed in on the driver's side. I carefully pulled out, getting a feel for Luke's truck. It wasn't all that different from my own.

I drifted into my own thoughts for a few moments as I headed back to Luke's driveway. I hoped desperately that I could find the key that I had seen in Bobby Joe's hand. I didn't exactly want to break in. . . . When I glanced over at Luke, his head was resting against the window and he was fast asleep.

CHAPTER TEN

As I walked into the office Monday afternoon, I wondered where God drew the line between a little white lie and an outright fib. Chances were I was walking that line pretty closely. I clutched a small piece of paper in my hand tightly, almost afraid that someone would tear it from me. I nervously pulled open the heavy wooden door of the office and stepped inside.

Placing my note on the counter, I waited tensely as Coach Henry Jones himself looked it over. I stared blankly at the forged signature of my mother at the bottom which I had traced from another note from long ago that I had found with some old notebooks.

Coach Jones, in a very good mood, handed me the piece of paper that he had just filled out and signed. The football team had won their game away against Brookfield on Friday, and things like that always put Coach Jones in a pleasant mood on Monday. His hand closed over my original note and swept it up for filing. I took one last look at my forgery, turned my back on it, and walked out of the office. Then I all but fled down the hall.

I read my official note carefully, wanting to be sure that everything was perfect. There was my name—*Tricia Lakely*. There was a little check mark next to the word LEAVING and another next to the word EXCUSED. Under REASON, the word *funeral* was scrawled in tight cursive lettering. The initials *HJ* were scrawled in a tiny blank beneath it.

I took the steps two at a time as I headed back upstairs to Spanish class, trying not to trip over my long skirt. As I walked through the door, my eyes automatically sought out Luke's familiar form, even though I already knew that he wouldn't be there. I carefully placed my excuse on Mrs. Darwin's desk and patiently waited as she penned in her initials, giving me permission to leave.

I picked up the excuse, shifted the weight of the backpack

hanging on my right shoulder, and quickly exited the room. I darted down the stairs, slowing at the bottom to catch my breath. I forced myself to walk at a reasonable pace down Short Hall to the office. I handed Coach Jones the signed excuse with as much poise as I could muster, picked up a pen, and signed the leaving list. Then I walked out of the office and made for the door as quickly as possible.

Bursting through the double doors and down the steps into the crisp autumn air, I wanted to run across the grass to the parking lot. Instead I forced myself to walk down the sidewalk like a proper young lady. It was one of the hardest things I'd ever done. Adrenaline is not always your friend.

I unlocked the door and pulled it open, dumping my books into the truck as calmly as possible. As I turned out of the parking lot and pulled onto the main road, I tried not to press the gas too hard. The gray truck sitting motionless in the Pizza Hut parking lot was a very welcome sight. I eagerly put on the blinker and turned into the lot to park right next to it.

Luke was sitting in his truck, waiting for me. Leaving my books in my own truck, I stepped out, locked the door, and dumped the keys in my pocket. I rushed around the back of Luke's truck as the engine fired to life, pulled open the door, and hopped in. He knocked the truck into reverse and pulled out.

"You know," I muttered, "we're going to end up getting caught before all this is over."

Luke grinned. "Not if we're as careful as Aaron made you promise to be."

"I feel horrible," I sighed. "I would never forge my mother's signature."

Luke shrugged. "Me neither, but there was no other way to be sure that Bobby Joe wasn't at home."

"I don't like this new lying habit. I certainly hope I can ditch it when this is all over."

Luke laughed at me. "A bad habit or two might do you some good, Tricia."

"You're one to talk, Mr. Perfect," I shot back. "Next thing you know, I'll have taken up cursing."

"So? Might grow on you."

"I doubt it," I said levelly. "And it better not grow on you, either." A smile was tugging at the corners of Luke's mouth. Even though he was trying not to laugh at me, he was still asking for it. "Speaking of cursing, I have a bone to pick with you, Mister Benson. When we were at Roscoe Thompson's. . . ."

Bobby Joe Fink lived in the middle of the closest thing that Judsonville had to slums. I felt another twinge of pity tug at my heart as I remembered the way that he had looked at Steve's gold pocket watch. It was followed by that persistent reminder that the man was one of my murder suspects.

Luke parked in the same space right in front of the apartment that Bobby Joe had used Friday night when we had followed him. Luke pulled the key out of the ignition and looked at me.

I'm not sure if it was to reassure him, reassure me, or both, but it seemed like the right thing to do at the time, so I winked at him. Both of us got out of the truck and headed for the door with the tarnished bronze *12*.

I dropped to my hands and knees and started digging around under the bare bush. I couldn't find anything but a bunch of rocks that were piled around the base of the ugly, scraggly bush. It had to be here. . . . Suddenly my fingers ran across something odd. It didn't feel like the other rocks around it. I looked down sharply. It felt like . . . plastic.

I picked the thing up quickly. It was an ugly gray plastic lump. Staring at it incredulously, I turned it over in my hand. Sure enough, there was a tiny sliding door on the bottom. I slid it open, and a little silver key clinked into my palm. I began to chuckle.

"What?" Luke asked, straining to see what I had found.

"I didn't know people actually used these."

Luke squinted at the gray thing in my hand. "What is it?"

"A fake rock to hide your key. One of those things that you see in mail-order catalogs all the time but you don't think that anyone really buys."

Luke shrugged. "Guess he didn't want to carry his key with him. He's probably got enough school keys to keep up with without having to worry about this one. Besides," he said, looking at the run-down apartment building, "I doubt he's got much in there to steal."

I replaced the rock and stood up, key in hand. Sticking the key into the lock, I twisted it, heard a click, and pulled open the door. The light filtering into the apartment from the outside didn't noticeably brighten up the dim room. I reached my hand in and flipped on the light switch before stepping inside.

The room that we stepped into was not one that I would like to have in my home—even see on a regular basis. The kitchen was illuminated by a single, bare light bulb in the ceiling. The sink directly across from me was stacked with the morning's dirty dishes, some of which were chipped. The stove was decidedly beat up, but it and the counters were extremely clean. The floor tiles were dented, and there a was a small hole in the floor near the corner of the room.

To the right, the kitchen opened up into a tiny living room. The floor was covered with scraggly, extremely worn carpet that was somewhere between gray and green. An old recliner of the same questionable color sat in the corner, with stuffing coming out of some of the burst seams. There was a card table beside the chair with a small lamp atop it and several books stacked beside it. Right next to the only window, across from the old recliner, sat an ancient television set with two metal antennae protruding from the top of it. The shelf was bowed, warped by the chunky television's weight. On the bottom shelf of the cart sat an old VCR. *Home sweet home*, I thought dryly.

Luke and I snooped through the kitchen and the living room for quite some time, but we couldn't find anything that seemed to have any significance. The process of gathering information was becoming easier, though—Luke and I had each worked out a sort of method that made it a bit easier to pinpoint what was useful and what wasn't. We would probably both be experts at searching houses when this was all over.

After quite some time of searching, Luke and I met in the middle, having searched the entire area. "Ready to move back?" he asked.

I nodded, and we headed for the door at the back of the living room. This opened into a small bedroom with another door at the left of the room, which I assumed was the bathroom. As I took in the dim, cramped little room, I decided that the designer of this apartment building hadn't believed in wasted space or luxury at all. I moved to the nearby nightstand and flipped on the small lamp resting upon it, the only source of light in the room.

Even though there wasn't much space at all, Bobby Joe appeared to be a fairly neat person. There were no objects or articles of clothing on the floor at all, and everything seemed to have its place. Of course, Bobby Joe probably didn't have enough possessions to make all that much of a clutter.

A small, plain, metal bed stood against one wall. It was neatly made with a beautiful afghan draped over it. Just that one afghan seemed to make the drab little room a bit more cheerful. I supposed that the little things like the brightness of that afghan were what made the run-down apartment bearable for him. The nightstand beside the bed and a small dresser on the other side of it were the only furnishings in the room. A tiny closet stood open right beside the dresser, and a small electric heater was positioned between the entrance and the bed it pointed toward.

Luke headed for the dresser and started rummaging through the drawers. I went for the closet.

All of Bobby Joe's clothes hung neatly on a warped and bowed wooden pole. I dropped to my knees and looked for any boxes that might be stacked on the floor. There weren't any boxes, however, just a pair of ratty sneakers and a pair of nice, sort of dressy black shoes. That was it for the floor of the closet—two pairs of shoes.

I stretched up on my very tiptoes to inspect the shelf, trying to keep my balance in those clumsy high heels. The shelf contained stacks of books. Most were old and worn. Judging by the titles, I guessed that he had owned some of the books since childhood. I flipped through the books for a few moments until I was interrupted by Luke's voice.

"Hey, Tricia?"

"Hmm?"

"Come here for a sec." I turned and stepped over to the dresser. Kneeling down beside Luke, I looked into the open bottom drawer. "I think these are all his important papers," Luke said, picking up a tan filing folder.

We flipped through the papers, coming across Bobby Joe's birth certificate, social security card, car insurance, and other such documents. Luke's fingers stopped moving as they revealed a plain piece of white copier paper with figures scribbled on it in black ink. The familiar *RT 555-1596* was written across the top. Directly underneath was the number *43,872* followed by the date *Dec. 25.*

"I certainly hope that's not what he's got to have paid back by

Christmas," Luke said with wide eyes.

"That's a lot of money," I whistled. My eyes scanned the empty page, noticing another figure at the bottom of the page. "What's that?" I wondered out loud.

"What's what?" Luke asked.

"That," I replied pointing to the number at the bottom of the page: *50,000*

"I don't know," Luke replied.

I stood up, grabbed a pen from the top of the dresser, knelt back down again, and started rolling up my sleeve.

"What are you doing?" Luke asked.

"Making sure we don't forget those numbers," I replied.

"Don't write on your arm again, Tricia," he protested.

I raised an eyebrow. "Would you rather I wrote it on your forehead?"

"Well, no. . . ."

"We have to write it down somewhere."

"Won't it be hard to wash off?" he asked.

I gave him an odd look. "I'll manage," I answered, starting to copy the figures onto my arm. "What's in the top drawer?"

"Oh, just the usual. Socks, underwear—"

"I get the picture," I broke in hastily. "Second drawer?"

"Pictures and such."

"Anything interesting?"

"Nah. Looked like family to me."

I got back to my feet and headed back toward the closet. "Hey, Luke?"

"Yeah?"

"What was Bobby Joe wearing the Friday of Homecoming?"

"Same thing he always wears on Friday," Luke replied promptly. "A Carrier High sweatshirt. The homemade one with the white Mustang right in the middle."

"Gotcha," I nodded. I rummaged through the closet but couldn't find the shirt. "It's not there," I told him as I turned away from the closet. We searched the bathroom, but I didn't find anything in there except the normal towels, soap, toilet paper, and such. We'd covered the whole house and hadn't come across that sweatshirt.

Where was it? I stood in the bathroom doorway for a moment, staring moodily out at the room. Just then, a box shoved under the bed caught my eye.

I jumped over to the bed, dropped to my knees, and pulled out the box. Inside was the sweatshirt. The first thing about it that caught my eye was the big dark red spot on the white horse's face in the center of the sweatshirt. I had a sinking suspicion that I knew what that red spot was.

"Luke!" I hissed, holding the shirt in limp fingers. He scrambled over to my side. I heard a sharp intake of breath as he looked at the sweatshirt.

"It's him," I whispered with disbelief.

"Wait," Luke countered. "How do you know that didn't happen when he found the body?"

"No," I said firmly. "He wouldn't have a reason to hide it. It's him."

"But we have to be able to prove it," Luke reminded me.

I stared down at the sweatshirt, running my finger across the stain of Paul's blood. "Wait," I whispered. "I think I *can* prove it!"

CHAPTER ELEVEN

It had been torture having to wait overnight to talk to Aaron and Joe. I sat down across from Aaron, and Luke automatically sat down next to me. "So," Aaron greeted us, "I see you're still alive."

"Yes," I replied, calmly as possible.

Aaron must have known something was up. He didn't even pretend to be interested in the lunch on the table in front of him. "You found something important, didn't you, Tricia?"

I nodded mutely, emotions boiling over inside. "I . . . well, we. . . ," I stuttered, trying desperately to get straight to the point but failing terribly. "We found . . . I think. . . ," I wondered irritably why I couldn't even make myself speak. Aaron had that deer-in-the-headlights look. He knew what was coming. "I. . . ," I tried one more time. I couldn't do it. I looked pleadingly at Luke.

"We think we found him," Luke whispered.

"It's him?" Joe asked uncertainly.

Both Luke and I nodded.

"How do you know?" Aaron demanded apprehensively.

"We found the sweatshirt he always wears to the games on Friday in a box under the bed. It . . . uh . . . well it had blood all over the white horse. There was a piece of white fabric in the box. It looked like he was going to pull the bloody fabric off and fix the white horse so that no one would notice."

"You know," Joe said finally, in a dull tone of voice, "that's really sick. Why didn't the idiot just throw the darn thing away like a sane person?" Joe looked like he wanted to choke someone, someone like Bobby Joe Fink. I would have agreed with him, but at the moment I was trying not to throw up.

"He couldn't," Aaron replied in a deceptively calm voice. "He can't change anything. It was odd enough to see him in a new sweatshirt the week after the murder. He'll want his old one back by the next home game, before people start asking questions."

"How are we going to prove this?" Joe asked quietly.

I shrugged. "With the sweatshirt."

"What if Bobby Joe panics and throws out the sweatshirt?" Joe asked skeptically. "Or what if he repairs it, like you said you think he's going to?"

"He can't," Luke replied promptly.

"Why not?" Joe asked uncertainly. "What's to stop him?"

Luke grinned nervously. "He doesn't have it anymore."

Aaron's eyes narrowed sharply. "You didn't!"

I shrugged. "We didn't have a choice. He might have destroyed the evidence."

"Tricia!" Aaron protested. "When he realizes it's gone, he's going to get desperate!"

"And then we're going to nail him, aren't we?"

"Where is it?" Aaron asked.

"In a safe place at my house," I whispered, not caring to broadcast the information to anyone nearby who was trying to act like he wasn't paying attention. This whole discussion was risky enough as it was.

Joe shook his head. "Just the sweatshirt won't prove anything. He might have gotten that blood on the sweatshirt when he found the body."

"I have an idea," I spoke up quickly. "Remember you guys said that you took a bunch of pictures before and after the game? I need to see all those pictures—every last one."

"Why?" Joe asked, confused.

"I need to see if there are any chance shots of Bobby Joe anywhere in there."

"I have a videotape my older brother made, too," Joe offered.

"Good," I said. "Can we get together tonight and look over this stuff?"

Aaron, Joe, and Luke exchanged a look.

"Yeah," Aaron replied promptly.

"Me too," Luke answered.

"My parents are going out tonight," Joe said slowly. "I'm supposed to stay home and watch my little brother, Robbie." Suddenly his face brightened. "Wait! Why don't we just get together at my house?"

Joe's house was more like a mansion, in my opinion. I checked the address and name on the mailbox about a dozen times before pulling up the driveway. I spotted Luke's gray Chevy, parked along the circle behind Aaron's little green car. It seemed that I was at the right place, after all.

I stepped out of my blue truck, feeling a bit like Alice in Wonderland. How was I supposed to know that Joe Taylor was rich? I took a deep breath, reminding myself that this was just Joe, the same guy that I argued with over lunch.

I marched right up to the front door and knocked assertively. The huge wooden door opened, and in the doorway stood a little boy who looked like he was about ten or so. "Hi!" I smiled warmly. "Are you Robbie?"

"Yeah," he replied easily. "And you're Tricia, right?"

"Right," I nodded.

The little blond boy thrust out his hand. "Pleased to meet you."

I took his hand and shook it. "Good to meet you too, Robbie."

Just then, I heard a commotion from the top of the stairs. "Hey, Robbie!" Joe's voice carried downstairs. "Is that Tricia?"

"Yeah!" Robbie called back up to the second floor. Then he turned to me and said, "Come on in."

"Thanks," I replied, stepping inside. I almost hesitated to step on the beautiful, polished hardwood floor in the foyer.

Suddenly, Joe's form appeared at the top of the steps. "Hey, Tricia!" he greeted. "Come on up." I bent down to untie my shoes. "Don't bother with your shoes," Joe said. "Just come on up."

"Hold up a minute," I replied firmly, despite his impatience. I knew the guys were all waiting on me, but I refused to tramp up that beautiful carpet in my sneakers. "I'll get the carpet dirty."

"I don't care!" Joe replied. He sounded like he'd had a bit too much caffeine.

"I do." I left my sneakers by the door and darted up the stairs. "See ya later, Robbie," I smiled back over my shoulder. Robbie smiled back. He looked like a good kid.

Joe led me to his room, where Luke and Aaron were sprawled out on his bed. Joe vaulted onto the bed, and I sat down on the floor near Luke, at the foot of the bed. "You can sit on the bed too, you know," Joe offered.

"Nah," I replied. "Rather just sit here and leave the high and lofty positions to the big men," I said with a smirk.

"Ha ha," Joe said dryly. "Then let's get down to business."

Aaron held out two envelopes of pictures. "I haven't looked through them again yet. I wanted to wait for you all." He handed me the pictures. "Go ahead, Tricia."

I carefully set the second envelope on the floor. Taking the first one, I pulled open the flap and took out the stack of photographs. I flipped through the pictures, my eyes focused for just one thing. All I saw were the familiar figures of the football team as they blurred past my eyes.

I stopped suddenly. "You didn't tell me about this one," I gasped as I pulled the picture out of the stack.

"Wanted to surprise you," Aaron grinned. "I knew you'd like that one."

I held up the photograph so that Luke could see it. Joe seemed to already know what it was—he was grinning too. There, in the photograph, stood Aaron, Joe, Steve Johnson, and two of the other players, Jared Hutchins and Tim Ketron. But the figure that caught my attention was the small form wearing a shy smile, right in the center with the guys' arms around his shoulders—none other than Bobby Joe Fink. His blue sweatshirt with the bright white cloth horse in the center was plainly visible.

"There you go, Tricia," Luke said. "That proves that Bobby Joe was wearing that sweatshirt at the game. Now you just need to prove that he wasn't wearing it when he found Paul Sanders's body."

Easier said than done. But my instincts were clear on this one—there was no room for doubt.

I flipped through more pictures as Luke looked over my shoulder, sprawled at the foot of the bed. I finished with the before-game shots, moving into the after-game photos.

"Whoa, wait," Luke said just as my hand froze. The picture was of Aaron and Joe. But in the background, walking the track all alone, was Bobby Joe. "He's still in his blue sweatshirt, though," Luke pointed out.

"Look, though, you guys," I said, pointing at the picture as they all moved closer. "You two are on the field facing the north end of the field. Bobby Joe is on the track, and he's headed toward the home stadium. He could be going to the men's bathroom. You never know. His chances of getting caught at this point would be slim because the only people who were left were family members, and all of them were on the field. The fans were gone, and no one would be in the bathrooms really. No one uses those bathrooms unless they have to."

"True," Luke agreed.

I flipped eagerly through more pictures. "There!" I cried triumphantly. "That's a gray sweatshirt, not a blue one, and that's definitely Bobby Joe, walking back the other way." I passed the picture around so that everyone could see. "Let's see that video now, Joe," I suggested, putting all the pictures away except for the two with Bobby Joe Fink in them.

Joe reached over and grabbed a black remote control from its resting place atop his nightstand. He pointed it at the TV across the room and punched buttons until the screen was blue and the word *play* was at the top right corner in little white letters. I waited nervously as the squiggly lines distorted the picture that Joe was fast-forwarding through.

The before-game coverage was over and soon the picture had lapsed into the last few minutes of the game. The lines disappeared as the movement slowed into the normal play mode with a red flash from the tip of Joe's remote control.

The emotions churned within me as I relived those hard moments. I saw the ball slip once again through Jared Hutchins's open fingers as Aaron's hand closed around the jersey beside him. I heard the crowd's cry of disappointment as the eleven blue jerseys moved ten yards back down the field. I felt a fresh wrench in my stomach as number 99 followed his teammates, hanging his head.

I could barely stand it. I glanced at Aaron out of the corner of my eye. His expression was grim and his eyes glued to the television screen. This was a night none of us probably cared to remember.

My focus returned to the screen as Tim Ketron came down with a pass that sent the people around the camera surging to their feet. I watched closely as both teams lined up along the line of scrimmage and—

"Wait," I said quickly. "Rewind it a tad!" Aaron was suddenly sitting rigidly upright behind me. "Did you see that, Aaron?" I asked.

"I think so. . . ."

Joe hit PLAY. There it came again. There was no mistake about it. There was no false start. There was a dead ball foul committed, but it wasn't a false start. Rather it was the defensive player who had jumped first—not Aaron. Number 99 marched up to the referee, and as I saw his mouth form the words "he moved first" once again, I knew this time that he had been right. Paul had made a mistake—the call should have been offside against the defense.

A million new, jumbled thoughts raced through my head as the video tape rolled onward. I continued to drown myself with what-ifs and speculation until Luke's voice pulled me out of my trance and back into reality. "Hey look!"

My head jerked up as Bobby Joe Fink moved across the screen, walking on the track toward the home bleachers, still in his blue sweatshirt. Not far ahead of him was the striped form of Paul Sanders with his black duffel bag slung over his shoulders.

"What's the number on the counter?" I asked quickly.

"Twenty-four, twenty," Joe replied promptly.

I nodded. The minutes dragged by as we waited impatiently for Bobby Joe to reappear, not really listening to what Joe, Aaron, and the other guys were saying. The counter read 32:16 when he returned wearing the gray sweatshirt. "He was gone about eight minutes," I said. "Plenty of time to walk in the bathroom, knife Paul, clean up, and change shirts."

"Just one problem, though," Luke put in. "What did he do with his other shirt?"

"Maybe he put it in the janitor's closet right by the men's bathroom," Aaron offered.

"Okay," Luke nodded, "but where did he get the gray sweatshirt? I've never seen him wear any Carrier High stuff except for his old blue sweatshirt."

Aaron shrugged. "That I don't know."

The machine buzzed as the tape began to rewind—the only sound for a few uncomfortable moments.

"I think Luke should keep the photos," Aaron said.

Joe nodded. "That's a good idea."

"Guess you're elected," I agreed, handing him the photos of Bobby Joe. "Is that it then?" I asked wearily.

"I think so," Aaron replied.

I felt my eyelids begin to droop as the room gave a lurch. I looked up at Luke, sitting cross-legged on the bed above me. Without a word, I leaned my head against his knee and closed my eyes. I had never felt so exhausted in my whole life.

The next thing I knew, Luke was giving me a gentle nudge, saying, "Tricia . . . wake up, Tricia." I was curled up against a vehicle door, and the seat belt was starting to cut into my neck.

"Hmm?" I muttered, opening my eyes. I was sitting on the passenger side of my truck. "Where are we?" I managed.

"Home," he replied.

As I looked up, sure enough, we were parked in my driveway. I saw a pair of low-beam headlights in the rearview mirror. "What's that?"

"Aaron," Luke replied. "He followed us. He's going to take me back to Joe's to pick up my truck."

"I must have fallen asleep," I observed, my mind still not completely awake.

"Yeah," Luke agreed. "You sure did."

I sat up and unbuckled my seat belt as the door opened beside me. "Are you alive in there?" Aaron asked.

"Yeah," I answered. "At least I think so."

Luke pulled the keys out of the ignition and handed them to me. "Good night, Tricia." He climbed out of my truck. "Sweet dreams," he added with a boyish smile. Then he shut the door and headed back down the driveway to Aaron's car.

"Thanks, Aaron," I said gratefully as I stepped out of my truck and shut the door behind me.

"I guess you had a rough evening, huh?" Aaron smiled.

"Why do you say that?"

"Because if it was a good night, Luke wouldn't have had to carry you down the stairs." I stared at him blankly. "You didn't think you sleepwalked down the stairs, did you?" Aaron gave me a deliberate wink and turned to leave.

CHAPTER TWELVE

I really didn't want to get up. I didn't even want to move, much less actually stand up and walk. Against my better judgment, I threw off the covers, dangled my legs over the side of the bed, and sat up. I sighed. There was no avoiding it—I might as well just get it over with. The first few steps were always the hardest part of the whole day—unless you count conjugating irregular Spanish verbs in more tenses than you can count. . . .

The good thing about getting ready in the morning is that you don't have to think to do it. It's all automatic, so you really get another half-hour or so of sleep after you get out of bed if you count zombie time.

By the time I was running on all cylinders, I found myself dumping my books into my backpack and crawling up on my bed. I pulled the drawstring closed and sat there with my arms around the backpack, realizing that I was finally awake. I sighed as all the cares of reality came crashing back. I would have to carry these through the day until I could leave them at the foot of my bed again tonight.

My eyes fell on a photograph, taped just beneath the wall clock. I let go of my backpack, moved over to the wall, and carefully pulled off the picture. I stared into Paul's eyes, not quite knowing what to feel. His arm was around my shoulder, and his other hand held the spatula that he had been using to flip burgers when the picture was taken.

I remembered that day, when he had surprised me by throwing a party for my sixteenth birthday. Paul was such a sweet, caring person.

Was. . . . The word stuck bitterly in my brain. Bobby Joe Fink had a lot to answer for, and his day of reckoning was coming. I slipped the photograph into my wallet, slung my backpack over one shoulder, and marched resolutely through my bedroom door.

* * *

Aaron, Joe, Luke, and I sat around a lunch table discussing the gray sweatshirt. If we could figure out where it had come from, there wouldn't be any holes left in our story.

Aaron shook his head. "Even if we have the evidence, how are we going to get the cops to accept our theory? I mean, we'd probably have trouble just getting them to sit down and listen to us. And then, since we're kids, they'll pick it apart, and since I'm the prime suspect and you guys are my friends, they'll accuse you guys of trying to frame Bobby Joe Fink to cover for me. After all, no one would ever believe that a bunch of kids put together a better investigation than the cops."

"Point," Joe agreed glumly.

"Then we can't let them know that a bunch of kids put it together," Luke said simply.

"What?" I asked, confused.

"Why couldn't we just mail it in as an anonymous tip? I mean, they can run the tests on the shirt. There's no way to duplicate Paul Sanders's blood, and one of those pictures could prove that Bobby Joe Fink was wearing that shirt Homecoming night. The only thing that's missing is where the gray sweatshirt came from. If we can plug in that hole, then we can type up an anonymous letter, throw everything in a box, and mail it straight to Sam Buckson. Concrete evidence from an anonymous source. That would be pretty hard for him to ignore, wouldn't it?"

"It would be hard for me to ignore, but I'm not Sam Buckson," Aaron replied.

I started to say something, but the loudspeaker interrupted me. "Aaron Tyler, report to the high school office," Coach Jones's voice blared. It didn't sound cheerful at all. I had a bad feeling about this.

"You know, Aaron," I said, "I was just headed that way to sit in the hall. Think I'll go with you." I wasn't sure why I wanted to go with him—after all Aaron was a big boy, and he could walk to the office by himself. I guess you could call it instinct. Luke and Joe offered a good-bye, and a "see you after third," and Aaron and I walked toward the double doors that led from the cafeteria into the high school building.

We walked side by side through Short Hall, toward the office, only a few feet away. Aaron was reaching for the doorknob, when I jerked his hand back with a gasp. I pulled him urgently away from the door, out of sight from the window.

"What?" he asked, surprised.

"Aaron, there are cops in there."

I saw Jackie staring at us from down the hall. I turned and motioned for her to come join us. She jumped to her feet and came flying toward us.

"How many were there?" Aaron asked.

"Four, I think. They're not here for a casual afternoon cruise."

Aaron put his hand to his forehead. Realizing I still held the other one, I hastily let it go as Jackie approached. "What's going on?" she demanded shakily.

"I got called to the office," Aaron replied in a deceptively composed voice. "There are cops in there."

"No!" Jackie sobbed. After taking a look for herself, she flung herself into Aaron's arms. As he held her, his gaze met mine, and I could see his love for her in his eyes. Jackie looked up bravely. "No matter what happens," she said solemnly, "I know you're innocent. And someday, the whole world will know it."

Then she looked me straight in the eye. "I know that you guys didn't want to tell me, because you didn't want me to worry. But I know what you've been doing. Whoever's responsible for this, you, Joe, and Luke nail him."

Then Jackie turned around and kissed Aaron. Right in the middle of the hall. And it wasn't a short kiss, either. Inappropriate contact such as kissing was one of those annoying school rules that no one really got suspended for yet few dared to break.

I scanned the hall for teachers, but fortunately, none were about. Jackie's friends were staring from the intersection of Long and Short halls, however. I consciously turned my back to Aaron and Jackie and stepped between them and the peeping Toms down the hall. I heard Jackie's heels against the floor as she stepped back. I turned around about the same time Jackie did.

"Bye," she whispered to Aaron, and then she gave me a quick, emotional hug—one that I wasn't really expecting. Without another word, she walked away, back to the staring eyes at the intersection of the halls.

Aaron shook my hand, turned, and reached for the doorknob. "See ya around, Tricia," he said, by way of farewell. I could see the courage straining across his face as he turned the knob, and I knew that he was afraid. An inhuman strength surged across his face as he pulled open the door and bravely marched into the office to meet his fate.

I stared out of the window, unable to take my eyes from the scene in the parking lot below. We were in groups again, supposed to be translating a cultural lecture in our Spanish textbooks. At least Luke's book was open—I hadn't even touched mine since I got back to class from lunch. Both of our notebooks were opened to sheets of completely blank paper.

"What are they looking for?" I whispered to Luke for probably the millionth time. Sam Buckson was standing next to Aaron, and the other three cops—one of which was Tommy Hall—were searching his car very thoroughly. I felt Mrs. Darwin's gaze as she glanced at us. I knew that she knew we hadn't done any work, but I think that she was too worried about us to care.

Suddenly, one of the cops pulled a big black duffel bag out from under the driver's seat. As he unfolded it, I instantly knew what it was. I had seen it many times before—at Paul's house. It was his duffel bag, the one that he carried everything to the game in. And Tommy Hall had just pulled it out of Aaron's car.

"That's not fair!" I hissed savagely, trying not to raise my voice too loud.

"What is it?" Luke asked, confused.

"That's Paul's duffel bag. Probably hasn't been seen since the night he died."

"What's it doing in Aaron's car?"

"I'll give you two guesses," I growled. "But you'll only need one."

"Fink?"

"Who else would plant that in Aaron's car? He must be onto us."

I watched sourly as Aaron moved to the car and put his hands on the top of it. Sam Buckson checked him for weapons, took his hands from the car, and handcuffed them behind his back. I could see his mouth move as he read Aaron his rights. As Aaron was loaded into the backseat of a patrol car, I stood up and headed for Mrs. Darwin's desk.

I muttered something about needing to go to the ladies' room. Mrs. Darwin nodded, and I walked out. However, I didn't go to the bathroom. Instead I walked across the hall to Miss Gardner's typing class. The door was open, and Joe Taylor sat at the second computer, right across from the door. I stood there for a moment until he saw me out of the corner of his eye and looked up. I crossed my wrists in front of me so that he could see. He nodded back glumly.

I headed on down the hall to the U.S. History room. I knocked and asked to speak to Jackie. As she walked through the door, shutting it behind her, I could see the strain in her eyes. She knew what I was about to say, but she was holding up. And she relieved my fears about keeping my own composure—she looked me in the eye and she didn't cry.

By the time the last bell rang, I was ready to wring Sam Buckson's neck for being so gullible. I all but stormed out of the building and made straight for my truck. Since I could barely see straight, it wasn't surprising that my wallet dropped out of my hand and onto the pavement while I was attempting to dig my keys out of my pocket. The wallet snap flew open, and my picture of Paul blew out, skittering a few feet in the weak breeze. I bent down and snatched it up, afraid of losing it.

As I picked up my wallet, something in the picture in my hand caught my eye. The arm around my shoulder was covered with a sweatshirt. A gray one. I stared at the Carrier High sweatshirt incredulously. It stood out larger than life, right down to the yellow grease stain on the sleeve cuff on the other side of my head that had happened that very day.

I yanked my truck door open and hastily climbed inside. My head was ringing with the realization that I had found the last piece of the Bobby Joe Fink puzzle. I twisted the key a bit violently, and the engine obediently sputtered into life. I carefully backed out of my parking space and made my way through the crowded parking lot.

Luke and Joe appeared out of nowhere beside my truck. I could hear Luke through the window as he yelled, "What are you doing, Tricia?" I ignored him and turned onto the street. I didn't have any time to waste. I had to get to Bobby Joe's apartment fast, dig up that sweatshirt, and be gone before he could get back to catch me. As I hit open road, my foot sank harder and harder against the accelerator.

I was almost afraid that Bobby Joe had discovered what we'd

done and moved his key, but I found that ugly, fake rock in the same place, with the same little silver key inside. I thrust the key into the door, turned it, and yanked the heavy mass of wood open. I wasn't sure if the door had shut behind me or not, but I didn't really care. I stomped through the apartment toward his bedroom.

It almost jumped right out of the closet and into my hands. I jerked the gray sweatshirt from its hanger and stared at it. The words *Carrier High Mustangs* ran across the front in shiny blue letters. And there, on the sleeve cuff, was that telltale yellow grease stain. With a violent lurch, I pulled the wad of gray material to my chest, almost afraid that someone would tear it from me. I stood there for a moment while the room spun around me, and then reality flooded back with a start. I blinked, turned around, and sprinted for the door.

I do know that the door shut behind me the second time. I was pretty excited, and I'm surprised the slam I gave it didn't make the rickety old thing fall off its hinges. I bent down, dropped the key into the fake rock, and made for my truck like there was a river of hot lava on my heels. There might have been, for all I knew—I never looked back.

I did, however, see in my rearview mirror the black beat-up Ford Ranger pulling to a stop behind me with its blinker on as I shifted my truck into reverse. And I also saw the rather annoyed-looking janitor behind the wheel. At that point I started screaming something, but to this day I don't even know what I said—it was probably pure gibberish. I whipped my truck toward the black one. I stomped on the brake just short of Bobby Joe's front bumper, knocked the truck into drive, and stomped on the gas.

My insides began a tug of war as I watched Bobby Joe in the rearview mirror. I saw his hand smack the blinker off and his face get a lot clearer in the mirror as he gained on me. A blaring horn brought my attention back to the front. I gasped and swerved back into my lane as the driver of the white Camaro whizzed past, shouting insults out the window.

My foot pressed harder and harder against the accelerator as I whipped around curve after curve, wondering whether the next one would sling me off the road. I had never been this way before, and I had no idea where this road was leading. The truth was I didn't care, as long as it wasn't a dead end. Bobby Joe wasn't gaining anymore, but he was keeping up. He looked at me like I'd just run over his favorite kitty cat. I shuddered and tried to focus on driving.

My heart was determined to beat a hole through my chest, and all I wanted was to be able to breathe. "Just drive," I muttered. According to my driver's education teacher, who insisted that teenagers have poor reactions to intense driving situations, I probably should have already wrecked, but I was hanging in there. I wasn't quite sure how I was still stuck to the pavement and not buried in the grass, but I didn't really want to think about it at the moment.

I watched uneasily as Bobby Joe's right hand left the wheel and reached across the seat. I couldn't be sure, but I thought he was rummaging around in his glove compartment. When his hand reappeared it was holding something small and black. I stared for a moment until his hand shifted on the wheel and I could get a good look at it. "Oh dear God!" I shrieked, my blood running cold. It was a gun.

I started screaming again as my eyes took in a DEAD END sign, just ahead. I spotted a little road branching off to the right. I yanked the wheel around, pouring on as much speed as I could handle as soon as I had made the turn.

I tensed and prayed as quickly as the words would come as Bobby Joe shifted the gun to his left hand and moved it out the open window. There was nothing on either side of the road but trees, an occasional cow, and a few empty fields—no one to hear me scream. . . .

I ducked as he squeezed the trigger. The shot went into the brush on the side of the road. I didn't have a clue what he was aiming for. If it was me, he sure was a horrible shot. I watched as he leaned forward and pointed his gun low—he was aiming for my tire. I swerved as he fired, and the shot missed. If he blew my tire, he could do whatever he liked to my truck and disguise it as an auto accident. No one would ever know . . . except for Luke, Joe, Aaron, and Jackie. But who would ever believe them?

My foot was nearly against the floorboard as it was, but I pressed harder, hoping against hope that I could lose him. He knew that I had the sweatshirt, and he would do anything in his power to stop me. A familiar sight opened up before me.

"Yes!" I shrieked, recognizing a familiar street. I made a quick left onto the street that wound around to run between the school and the stadium. He was right on my tailgate, but his arm was inside, and the gun was nowhere in sight. I smiled nervously as the traffic moving in the other direction poured past.

On impulse, I made a quick right and drove through the open gates and into the stadium. I flew onto the track and drove around the familiar oval, the black Ranger not far behind. I had him now. I could circle the track forever if I wanted to, or at least until someone noticed me.

I spotted Luke over in the school parking lot and laid on the horn, hoping to get his attention. He looked up, caught sight of me, and ran across the street toward the stadium. I looked up just in time to see Bobby Joe reach out the window, gun in hand.

And then he did what I had least expected him to do right in the middle of Judsonville—he fired. My front tire blew, sending me careering violently off the track. I stomped the brake, steering wildly away from the quickly approaching concrete stadium. My truck jerked to a stop, just shy of slamming into the corner of the field house.

I ripped off my seat belt, grabbed the sweatshirt, nearly broke my hand throwing open the door, and scrambled outside. I sprinted around the back corner of the field house, ducking away from the gun pointed at my back. I ripped open the back door, vaulted myself inside, and fell right into Steve Johnson— who happened to be wearing nothing but a towel. Fortunately for me, the towel was in a very strategic location.

"Tricia!" a very startled Steve managed as I grabbed for the doorknob and turned the lock. "What in the name of . . . of thunder . . . are you doing in here?"

Normally I would have appreciated the fact that he made the effort to make an alternate word choice, but at the moment I barely noticed.

"He's after me!" was all I could manage.

Just then Joe appeared, also wearing a towel around his waist. "Tricia! What's going on?"

I held up the gray sweatshirt.

"Where did you get that?"

"Apartment," I gasped. "He's after me!"

"Here?" Joe demanded.

"He's outside. He's got a gun, Joe. He shot out my tire."

Steve Johnson did swear this time. "What's going on here?"

"For heaven's sake—lock the doors, Joe!" I pleaded. Joe turned and made for the front, and Steve Johnson ran to the end of the hall and locked the side door.

Just then, Coach Jones appeared. His eyes widened as he caught sight of me. "What in tarnation are you doing in here, girl?" he demanded. "You can't be in here!"

"Sorry, Coach Jones," I babbled, "I couldn't help it . . . he's after me with a gun, and he shot out my tire, and there was nowhere else—"

"What? What's going on?"

Just then a loud pounding from the front door broke through the commotion. "Tricia Lakely!" came a shout from outside. I turned away from Coach Jones and ran up the hallway.

"If you don't want it seen, cover it now!" I screamed for the benefit of anyone in the main room. I could hear a great deal of shuffling around as I entered the room. Most of the guys were at least partially dressed, but a couple had grabbed for the nearest object they could get their hands on. Everyone looked more than a little surprised to see me. At the moment I didn't really care.

I went straight for the door. The shout came again. "Get out here, Tricia Lakely! Get out here or he dies!"

I froze. "What?" I called back.

"I've got your friend. Get out here or he dies!"

"You're lying!" I shouted back frantically.

"Tell her!" I heard Bobby Joe command.

"Um, Tricia?" My knees threatened to buckle at the sound of Luke's trembling voice.

"Luke?"

"I'm sorry, Tricia."

"Where are you?" I asked desperately.

"Right outside the door."

"I've got him!" Bobby Joe hollered again. "Get out here with the shirts or I swear I'll kill him!"

"Why?" I screamed. "Then you'll get caught for sure!"

"They won't believe you anyway, you know," Bobby Joe cried desperately.

"Just let him go!"

"Give me the shirts!"

"I don't have them both with me!" I protested.

"You'd better come up with them, considering I've got three bullets left."

"I'm in here," I pointed out.

"But your friend's out here with a gun to his head," he shot back.

Just then I heard the sound of sirens. Someone had called the cops. Thank goodness—maybe.

"Now you've gone and brought them into it! I swear if you don't open that door this moment, I'll take him with me! I'll blow his brains out! One. . . ."

"Wait!" I shrieked. I jerked the lock open.

"No, Tricia!" Joe leapt forward to pull me back, but I had already yanked the door open. Luke was on his knees beside the tall, skinny janitor, the black gun pressed against the side of his head, staring hopelessly at me.

"Which is it going to be, girl? You or him?"

"No, Tricia," Luke whispered.

"Shut up, boy!" Bobby Joe snapped.

The sirens grew louder and louder as the police cars pulled onto the track.

"It's over," I insisted. "They'll shoot you if they see you with that gun! It's too late now."

"Wait!" Bobby Joe protested. "It wasn't my idea to kill him! What do I care about a referee? I just needed money—"

"Drop the gun!" came the voice of Sam Buckson.

"I can tell you who hired me," he pleaded.

My eyes narrowed. "Just drop the gun. It's finished."

"No, not yet," he said.

Then a gun went off. "NO!!" I shrieked as Luke's body shuddered. He couldn't die—not like this!

But it was Bobby Joe who fell, his gun clattering to the ground. The shot hadn't come from his gun, and it hadn't come from the police. It had come from the rock face behind the stadium. Atop it stood a figure dressed in black. The figure lowered the gun, turned, and ran out of sight.

Without further hesitation, I jumped from the field house and dropped to my knees in front of Luke. He was still staring at me, trembling. I threw my arms around his shoulders, pulled him close, and before I could stop to think, I leaned forward and kissed him.

He pulled away after a long moment and stared into my eyes. "Tricia," he gasped. And then he wrapped his own arms around me and kissed me back, as if to be sure I was real and he was still alive.

When my eyes finally opened, there were cops all around us. I reluctantly pulled away from Luke and stood up. I looked down at the limp form of Bobby Joe Fink, blood trickling from his lifeless lips. He stared up at me vacantly and yet almost accusingly.

I turned away, feeling more than a little nauseated. I had sworn long ago that I could have no sympathy for a murderer. Bobby Joe had thrown his life and Paul's away for money, and I knew that I should hate him, but I couldn't stop the tear from running down my cheek. My compassion had forced me to give one tear to Bobby Joe Fink. But as I turned away, Luke's hand clutched protectively in mine, I knew that that was all he would ever get from me. One tear.

CHAPTER THIRTEEN

It was nice to be in the chairs this time, instead of under the table. This was only my second time in Coach Jones's office, and I liked this viewpoint a lot better than the one from the floor. Sam Buckson was pacing the room like a cougar with a stomach ache. I idly wondered how long he could keep up that strenuous pacing before either his feet fell off or he passed out. Luke and I sat side by side, staring at the pictures on the wall, waiting for some sound other than Sam's shoes against the floor to break the silence.

I sat up straight as I heard the door open behind me. I glanced over my shoulder to see Joe Taylor enter, followed by Coach Jones. Coach Jones made his way to his chair behind the desk, and Joe seated himself on a clear corner of the wooden table in the corner. Sam Buckson paced his way over to Coach Jones's desk and stopped.

"All right, then," Sam said after a long pause. "Now that we're all here, let's get started."

All? Not entirely accurate, I thought. Especially considering that Paul was long dead, Aaron was locked up in a cell somewhere, Bobby Joe Fink was being scraped up off the track outside, and we didn't even know who the gunman in black was.

"Now, it is true that you have the Constitutional right not to answer my questions if you don't want to, but it would be to your great advantage to talk to me."

"We don't have anything to hide, Mr. Buckson," I replied calmly.

"All right, Miss Lakely," Sam said, focusing his gaze on me. "Let's start with you. You seem to be right in the middle of all this. Would you like to start at the beginning?"

I took a deep breath. "Which beginning? A lot's happened in the past few weeks."

"What was going on between you and Mr. Fink?"

I figured that I might as well get straight to the point. "We discovered that he killed Paul Sanders, and he tried to stop me from delivering the evidence to the police." ʻ

Henry Jones whistled. "Somehow I think that's the end more than the beginning, girl," he noted.

"True," I agreed with a shrug. "But that was the simplest answer to his question."

"What evidence?" Sam asked quickly.

"We have pictures of Bobby Joe Fink on the night of the murder. Before and during the game, he was wearing a blue sweatshirt with a white cloth Mustang in the center. He wears it every Friday, and we have a picture of him that night wearing it. Sometime that night he changed into this." I held up the gray sweatshirt.

"We also have pictures of him in this after the game," I continued. "You will find the initials *PS* on the tag. And this yellow grease stain on the sleeve"—I pointed to the stain—"matches the one in a picture I have of Paul Sanders, wearing this shirt. The blue sweatshirt has a large bloodstain on the white cloth horse, and if you test it, I believe you will find it to be Paul Sanders's blood.

"We also have a video made the night of the murder in which Bobby Joe Fink can be seen in the background first walking toward the men's bathroom where the murder was committed, and then away from it again. He was gone for approximately eight minutes. When he left, he was in the blue sweatshirt, and when he came back he was in the gray one. We have it all on tape—and in pictures."

"How did you obtain this evidence, Miss Lakely?"

"The pictures and videotape belong to members of the team. They were lent to me."

"And the sweatshirts? You have both in your possession, correct?"

"Yes," I replied uncomfortably. I knew what he was getting ready to ask me.

"You haven't been doing any breaking and entering, have you, Miss Lakely?"

There was the bombshell. Luke gave me a nervous glance. Perhaps it wasn't just Aaron's tail on the line, after all. "Just a second, there Mr. Buckson. Let's back up a second," I said. "Did you hear what Bobby Joe said before he was shot?"

"When we arrived, you were telling him to drop the gun, that it was finished."

"And then what did he say?" I asked again.

"He said that it wasn't his idea—that he didn't care about a ref. Then he said something about needing money, and he said he could tell you who hired him."

"And then he got shot."

"Tommy wrote the whole conversation down word for word. I just don't have it with me."

"So," I said, "would you call that a confession?"

"Depends on how you look it. We hadn't arrested him or brought him in for questioning—"

"You know what I mean. Do you agree that he was admitting that he killed Paul Sanders?"

"It isn't 100%, but it pretty much sounded like that was what he was doing, didn't it?"

"So once you see that evidence I told you about, and accept that it's legitimate, taking that and what Bobby Joe said before he died, would you pretty much conclude that he's the murderer?"

"If the evidence was legit," Sam replied, "yeah, I'd say so."

"So what evidence did you have against Aaron?"

"We got the knife back. Some of the prints were smudged, but the only ones identified belonged to Aaron, and the blood was definitely Paul Sanders's. Then we got an anonymous tip that Mr. Sanders's sports bag was hidden in Aaron's car. So we searched it, and found it."

"My guess," I replied, "is that Bobby Joe caught on to us and planted the bag in Aaron's car without his knowledge."

"How long have you been working on this case, Miss Lakely?" Sam asked, his eyebrows doing something really weird. I guessed that the curiosity was getting to him.

"Since the morning I found out that Paul was dead, and that Aaron's knife killed him."

"May I ask why?"

"Because Paul was my friend," I replied slowly, looking straight into Sam Buckson's eyes. "I wanted to know what happened to him and why. Aaron is also a friend of mine, and I knew that he wasn't capable of murder. So I decided to find out what really happened."

"So, back to the obtaining of the evidence. You managed quite a change of subject, didn't you, dear?"

"I was making a point."

"And the point is . . . ?"

"That Bobby Joe Fink killed Paul Sanders, and we solved the murder."

"Just a sec, little lady. We haven't seen that evidence yet."

"Look, what he said is pretty good evidence, plus I promise you'll get your evidence as soon as possible. Do you think I made all this stuff up on the spot? Besides, how else would you explain the fact that he was trying to kill us?"

"All right. For the moment we'll assume that Bobby Joe Fink killed Paul Sanders, and you solved the murder."

"I think now's the time for a little bargain."

"What kind of a bargain?" Sam asked suspiciously.

"Say, we give you the evidence, murder solved, and you sorta don't prosecute us for any laws we might have broken while obtaining the evidence."

"No murder, I hope?"

"No." I smiled.

"No illegal drugs, no assault and battery, no sabotage?"

"More along the lines of breaking and entering."

"About what I figured. Is that all?"

"Unless you count speeding while Bobby Joe tried to shoot my tire out."

"Well, I think we can handle that in exchange for the evidence."

"So you'll give *all* of us immunity?"

"How many of you does this apply to?"

"Just two."

"You and Mr. Benson?"

"Yeah."

"All right. If you hand over the evidence, we don't prosecute you."

"Let's shake on it," I said.

"All right." Sam extended his hand. First I shook it, and then Luke did. "So," Sam continued conversationally afterward, "how many times did you indulge in this breaking and entering?"

"Oh, I don't know. . . ," I shrugged.

"Four or five, or so," Luke said. "Give or take a couple, depending on your point of view."

Sam seemed surprised. I felt like laughing in his face. We'd managed to outdo both him and the murderer at their own game. One of the murderers, anyway. The other one still worried me, though. He was even more dangerous than Bobby Joe Fink, and he was definitely smarter and a lot more underhanded than Bobby Joe could even have dreamed of being.

"You've all been quite busy, haven't you?" Sam noted. "Still, I'd be curious to know how you uncovered this all so quickly."

"Well, Mr. Buckson, we have certain advantages over cops."

"Such as?"

"To get a warrant, you guys have to know exactly what you're looking for. Plus it takes time. We just snooped. You have strict rules that don't always apply to us. Besides, people tense when they see cops. But who pays any attention to a bunch of kids? Heck, we wouldn't know what to do with evidence if we stumbled across it and got it shoved in our faces, right?"

Sam just stared at me. If he thought all teenagers were stupid, he had another thing coming. Tommy Hall wasn't quite as shocked, however. He knew better. He had his own teenage daughter.

"If you don't mind my asking, why was Aaron your only suspect?" I asked curiously.

"We were working with the professional aspect of Mr. Sanders's life, and the only solid leads we had led to Aaron Tyler." He looked at me for a moment. "What do you think Fink's motive was?"

"Money. He was hired."

"But why was he so desperate for money?"

"Because he owed Roscoe Thompson $43,872, which had to be paid back by Christmas. There was a figure at the bottom of the page that read 50,000. I can only assume that that's what the second party paid him for the job."

"That's not a lot of money for a murder."

"But it was enough. Bobby Joe Fink probably didn't even know the difference. He didn't necessarily have the biggest dose of common sense in the world. He shot my tire out in the middle of the stadium, for crying out loud."

"Well, this other guy is our problem now. I want you to stay out of this, Miss Lakely. Now that this guy knows you are involved, he's gonna have his eye on you. The situation could become dangerous. I want all of you just to get on with your lives and forget about all this. Leave the rest to us. We'll do fine without more help, and we can't promise any more immunity if you break the law again. That goes for all of you. For you, Tricia Lakely, for you Luke Benson, and for you, Joe Taylor, even though I don't know what your part in all of this has been. And that will go for Aaron Tyler, too."

Coach Jones gave us a stern look. "This is serious business, and it's no place for kids. Y'all are lucky you're still alive. You don't need to be mixed up in this stuff. And you remember what I said, Joe Taylor. You and Aaron keep your noses out of trouble. And stick to school and football."

"What about Aaron, Mr. Buckson?" Joe asked quickly. "Can he go now? I think the blind rage theory just went out the window."

"Yes," Sam sighed. "It did. The law states that he can be held for forty-eight hours after arrest before being charged. Since he hasn't been charged, he'll be released, and that'll be the end of it for him, hopefully. Now you kids head on out of here. We've got work to do, and you've got lives to get back to."

"When can we expect Aaron back?" Joe asked.

"I'll call and have them drive him down here now."

"Good luck, Mr. Buckson," I said, extending my hand as I stood up. Sam hesitated but shook it. After all, a bunch of kids had just done his job for him. I didn't really expect him to consider it a pleasure working with me. More like a nuisance, probably. At least he had the killer, though.

Only, the killer had just been killed.

I turned and walked out of the room, followed by Luke and Joe. The light was blinding as we stepped outside. The ambulance was there, and a motionless lump covered with a white sheet was being lifted from the pavement and loaded on a stretcher. Yellow caution tape was being put in place around the scene, and I could see a crowd of people armed with cameras, video and otherwise, pouring into the stadium.

Football players were trickling out of the stadium and making for their cars, trying to get away from the mess. I wondered how many were glad to get out of practice, how many thought it was a shame to miss with a big game coming up, and how many just didn't care as long as they could get away from the reporters, the cops, the paramedics, and the mess on the track.

Me, I just wanted out. I was pretty sure that Luke and Joe felt the same way. We had a friend to wait for.

We slipped out the back gate, unnoticed. I smiled. We were free, and we could just leave the reporters for Sam Buckson. It was part of his job, after all.

CHAPTER FOURTEEN

"So what are we going to do now?" Joe asked. "I know we were going to wait for Aaron, but if we stay here, we're going to end up getting attacked by reporters. I don't know about you guys, but I don't feel up to dealing with those guys right now, and I haven't even been shot at today."

"Really," I sighed. "Look. Why don't we run and get that stuff for Sam Buckson? I don't want to leave that for later—the sooner he's got it, the better, don't you think?"

"I agree," Luke replied quickly. "Whoever shot Bobby Joe got a good look at both Tricia and me, and I don't want him after me. If he wants the evidence, let him shoot at Sam Buckson. He's used to getting shot at, and at least he can fight back." With that Luke pulled open the driver's side door of his gray Chevy and climbed inside. "Coming?" he called through the open passenger side window.

"Well, yeah," I replied, opening the passenger side door, "unless you plan to forget everything Sam Buckson just told you and go break into my house."

"I think I'd rather take you with me, in that case," Luke replied.

"Wait a sec," Joe said, as he jumped in after me, shutting the door behind him. "You mean it's in your house?"

I sighed. "Where else did you want me to put it, Joe? In the bed of my truck?"

"Well, no, but wasn't that putting yourself in a lot of danger?"

"No more than I would have been in anyway. It's not like anyone knew it was at my house. It could just as easily have been at your house, or Luke's house, or Aaron's house, or even Jackie's house for all anybody knew. Besides, I don't think that until today Bobby Joe fully understood how much evidence we had against him."

"So now what are we going to do?" Luke asked.

"If I were you, I'd make a left right here onto Horizon Drive."

"You know what I mean," Luke protested as he flipped on the left blinker. "Whoever that gunman was, he knows that you and I are somehow involved, so we have to play this carefully."

"He might not know about Aaron and me," Joe said thoughtfully. "And that might give us an advantage, but then that sort of balances out with the fact that Coach Jones and all the other assistant coaches are going to be watching us like hawks. We're going to really have to watch what we do."

"Okay," I said. "The first thing we have to decide is if we're really going to leave this to the police like Sam Buckson told us to."

Joe laughed.

"Yeah, right," Luke chuckled. "When, since Homecoming, have we done anything the adults in charge told us to?"

"Well, I don't know about you," I laughed, "but I'm still in the habit of turning in my Algebra homework when Mrs. Cleary asks for it."

"Okay, you win. But how often have we done what Sam Buckson says?"

"You win that one, Luke. But we're kind of in a sticky situation here. If we start snooping, the killer will probably know it, but if we don't, he might suspect we are anyway, and that means we're still in danger. At any rate, the sooner this guy is caught, the safer for us."

"Yeah," Luke agreed. "Still, as long as we don't know for sure that he's onto Joe and Aaron," he continued, turning to Joe, "I think you two should pretty much watch this one from the sidelines."

"Wait just a minute!" Joe protested. "You can't just go getting into trouble and keep Aaron and me in the dark about all of it!"

"No, we'll keep you informed," I said. "But you guys had better stay out of it yourselves, and probably look like you don't even have a clue, even though you will."

"Sam Buckson's not going to be happy if we plop another solution in his lap," Luke muttered. "The police department's not going to want to admit that it was beaten out by a bunch of kids."

"What he does about spreading credit is up to him," I said. "I just want the man in black off my back."

"My, that was tongue twister."

"Shut up, Luke," I laughed as he pulled into my driveway. Mom was still at work, so there was no one home. I pulled my house key out of my pocket and marched up to the front door. I didn't bother with the front light, but ran straight down the hallway to my room. After flipping on my little bedside lamp, I dropped to my knees, lifted up a huge afghan, and pulled a box out from under my bed.

It wasn't that I wasn't creative enough to think of a better hiding place, it was just that I was getting comfortable with the whole under-the-bed thing, and hey—it worked for everyone else.

I opened the box and quickly went through the contents. Blue sweatshirt, videotape, photographs, the papers where we had copied the figures from Roscoe Thompson's and Bobby Joe Fink's files—yes it was all there. All but the gray sweatshirt, which already rested safely back at the field house with Sam. Even the little tape that held the recorded conversation of Sam Buckson and Tommy Hall was there.

I snatched up the precious box, jumped to my feet, and ran back down the hallway. I opened the door, stepped outside, and locked it behind me. Cramming the key in my pocket I headed back for Luke's truck and got in, exhaling a deep breath. "It's all here. Let's go."

Luke backed out of the driveway and onto Horizon Drive. As we headed back to school, I pulled the miniature cassette tape out of the box and shoved it into my pocket. I didn't necessarily want Sam Buckson or Tommy Hall coming across that helpful little clue.

"So here we are already breaking our promise to Sam Buckson to stay out of it," I sighed. "We're getting to be a bit immoral."

"Nah," Joe disagreed. "I don't see how we're breaking any promises."

"Well, maybe we're not snooping yet, but we're definitely conspiring to snoop."

"Ah, but you're forgetting the whole trick, Tricia. We never actually promised."

"What?"

"Sam Buckson told us to mind our own business all right, but we never promised to. Heck, we didn't even say okay, or whatever, or even acknowledge the command. So we're not breaking any promises."

"How do you do that?" Luke laughed.

"Do what?" Joe asked innocently.

"Get around promises like that? Tricia might be the world's best for not breaking promises, but you've got to be the world's best for not even making them, and making the opposite parties think you did to get them out of your hair."

Joe shrugged. "We all have our own special talents." He grinned.

My eyes stared through the windshield, even though I couldn't see a thing. My mind was elsewhere. "So now what?" I muttered. "Where haven't we looked? We didn't go too far into who could have a motive for killing Paul."

"Yeah, but that could take forever," Luke protested. "Didn't you hear Sam? The cops were working with motives, and they didn't get anywhere. They didn't even get out of his professional life and into his personal life. Who's to say we'd do any better?"

"We don't have a lot of elbow room now, though," I replied, my eyebrows creased. "This person didn't have to be physically able to kill Paul, and he didn't have to have access to the field house. He didn't even have to be at the game."

"Wait a minute," Joe said. "Sam Buckson said they were working with Paul's professional life. What did he do besides referee?"

"He was a deliveryman for Venny's Shipping Company."

"Any way we could get a list of his deliveries in the last few days before he was killed?" Joe asked.

"Maybe Sam Buckson's got a copy," I mused.

"Yeah, and I'm sure he'd just hand it over if you asked for it," Luke said sarcastically.

Joe shrugged. "Who says you gotta ask?"

As Luke drove slowly around the track toward the field house, I wondered if the reporters rushing at us, cameras flashing, were half English charger, thinking they were at a jousting tournament. I was certainly ready to call the mass of people flinging themselves at us a stampede.

"Drats!" Luke snapped. "I can't see!" Flashes were going off in all directions, and it seemed like thousands of video cameras with shiny red beams of light were aimed at us.

"Well," Joe replied mildly, "you can claim temporary physical incapacity or some such gibberish as defense when you run them all over."

"Honestly!" Luke shook his head. "Do they want to get flattened, or are they really good actors?"

"We'd get there faster walking," I pointed out.

Joe shook his head vigorously. "I don't think so."

Just then someone climbed into the bed of Luke's truck. "What's he doing?!" Luke exclaimed, glancing in the rearview mirror.

The crowd in front of the truck solidified and stopped moving, forcing Luke to pull to a stop. More people scrambled into the bed of the truck, and the cab started to rock with their movements. My perception of the crowd began to shift from charging horses to hungry crocodiles, swimming in circles to surround us in our quickly sinking boat.

Luke laid on the horn, and Joe and I motioned to the people in the back to get out of the truck. When we didn't get any reaction other than blank stares and flashing cameras, we turned back around and refused to look at them. Luke was obviously losing his patience. Just then an eager photographer grabbed the grill, lodged his foot on the bumper, and hauled himself onto the hood.

"I don't believe this!" Luke shouted, blaring the horn over and over again. "It's like attack of the killer ants or something!"

"Only these guys got cameras," Joe added.

Personally, I was seriously beginning to question if these people were even half human. "That's it," I said. "Joe, roll down your window."

"What?"

"Just do it."

"You're not going to scream in my ear, are you?" he asked cautiously as he began to wind the window handle on the door.

"Nope. You're going to do the screaming for me."

"What do you want me to say?"

"Tell them that all they're going to get is pictures until we get to field house. None of us are going to answer any questions until we take care of our business with Sam Buckson."

"Excuse me!" Joe bellowed out the window.

Not exactly how I would have started it—"Yo, dorks!" was more along my sentiments at the moment—but at least it got their attention.

"If you'll all please step aside, we have business at the field house!" No reaction. "Look, we're not going to answer any questions or give you people any kind of a statement until we take care of our business with the police first. So if you want your story, the smart thing to do would be to let us get on with what we need to do so that you can all get home sometime tonight. How does that sound?"

The crowd began to grudgingly disperse after that. Perhaps they were human, after all.

Luke pulled up beside my Toyota, resting crookedly on its flat tire. He cut off the engine, opened his door, and jumped out, locking the door behind him.

"Would you people please get out of my truck?" Luke begged the photographers who had hitched a ride in the bed of the truck. "You're going to scratch the paint."

As Joe and I scrambled out and locked our door, Luke sighed and turned his back on them. We walked briskly side by side toward the field house, leaving a mob of reporters milling around dejectedly on the other side of the caution tape. I had no idea that there were that many news agencies around a piddly little place like Judsonville. They must have come in from a really wide radius.

"And reporters wonder why they get a bad rap," Luke muttered under his breath.

We walked resolutely through the main room of the field house where Tommy Hall and another policeman were standing guard, then continued down the hall to the offices. We were going through the general office when an unfamiliar briefcase lying open on the desk caught my attention. The coat atop it was familiar though—maybe because Sam had been wearing it when he and the cops arrived.

"I think I'll wait here," Joe said as Luke and I moved for the door. I raised an eyebrow. Joe looked at the copying machine in the corner meaningfully and winked.

Luke and I went into Coach Jones's office, and Luke shut the door behind us, leaving Joe alone with Sam's briefcase and the copier.

Sam Buckson was waiting for us in Coach Jones's office. The coach himself was planted in his chair with his feet propped up on his desk. I handed Sam the box, grateful to finally be rid of it. "It's all in there," I said. "Everything I promised you."

"I'll look everything over," he assured me. "I'm sure it's all in order. That will be all."

"Coach Jones," I said tentatively.

"Yes?"

"It will be all right to leave my truck where it is for a couple of days won't it?"

"Of course."

"Good. Just checking."

"Mr. Buckson?" This time it was Luke who spoke. "There's no way you could sort of get the reporters off our backs is there?" he asked hopefully.

"Comes with the snooping," he replied—pretty unsympathetically, I might add.

"What do you want us to tell them?" I asked.

"Whatever you want," Sam replied, "but just remember that anyone will be able to see or read what you say, including the gunman. It's up to you how much you want to tell them. The reporters already know that you two are involved and were shot at, but that's all they know about you. The rest is up to you. I'd say the less the better, though, for your own safety."

Yeah, I thought as I nodded. *For our safety, and for the credit of Sam Buckson and the rest of the cops. They probably don't want this out to the press, either.* We turned to leave.

"Good luck, kids," Coach Jones called after us. At least *he* was sympathetic.

CHAPTER FIFTEEN

"Did you get it?" I whispered as we walked through the hall. Joe winked and pulled a wad of folded up paper out of his pocket. He handed it to me, and I shoved it into my own pocket as Joe pulled open the back door. We jumped out the back and slipped behind the away stands without seeming to attract any attention.

"I'm going to have to come back for my truck, you know," Luke whispered.

"I know, but there's nothing we can do about that," I replied.

"I'm parked in the gravel parking lot," Joe said. "We can go out the back gate, get in my car, drive across to the main parking lot, and wait for Aaron. Maybe if we're lucky, it'll take a while for the reporters to figure out what happened to us."

Luke and I nodded, and the three of us crept along the back of the stadium, sandwiched between the concrete and the rock of the cliff Walter Camp Field sat nestled up against. We didn't even pause at the corner of the stands before darting behind the little cheerleading building and then out the back gate. We wound our way through the lower gravel parking lot to the upper one, where Joe's red Mustang convertible was parked.

"Nice car," Luke noted appreciatively. "But why on earth did you park it over here in the gravels?"

Joe shrugged. "I usually park in the main lot, but I was running late this morning. So it was here or nothing." He retrieved his key from his pocket and unlocked the doors. "Hop in," he offered. Luke and I got in the back, and Joe climbed into the driver's seat.

Joe started up his nice, shiny Mustang and we rolled slowly out of the gravel parking lot and across the road to the main, paved lot. Joe pulled up along the end of the school behind the steps. Aaron's car was not very far away, so we could pull up when we saw him coming. But here, camouflaged by the brick school, we would attract less notice than we would out in the middle of an empty parking lot. Plus add in the factor that the reporters at the field house couldn't see us here—their view was blocked by the home stands. Now it was time to just sit tight.

It was so quiet. I stared out the window, and for the first time in a while, I was able to actually think. The day's events rushed through my head, from Aaron's arrest to my stupid escapade over at Bobby Joe's and the chase that followed. None of it seemed real.

Right now, I didn't want to be Tricia the hero or Tricia the spy. I just wanted to be Tricia the teenager, preferably a sleeping one. I don't really think Luke minded my head on his shoulder as I closed my eyes and my muscles relaxed, my troubles and tensions ebbing away. The last thing I felt was Luke's hand putting mine in his, and his other arm sliding about my shoulders before all the rest of the world faded into darkness.

The next thing I remembered was the shouting outside and the face in the window that brought me back to my senses. "Wha—" I mumbled, squinting against the flashing camera. I sat up, gripping Luke's hand even tighter. I wasn't sure why I was afraid of these people, but then, being cornered is never pleasant. I groaned. "Don't these people ever give up?" I sighed.

"I guess not," Joe replied wearily. "It's their job not to give up, I suppose."

I sighed again. "You might as well roll down the window, Joe."

He turned around to look at me. "What?"

"They're not going to go away until we tell them something."

"But I thought we decided not to tell them anything."

"We're not," I winked. "We're just going to say enough words to make them think we told them something."

Joe shrugged. "Your call, Tricia. We'll follow your lead." He moved the key forward a position in the ignition. "Just remember what we decided about Aaron and me staying out of it from here on out," he added, turning around again. "I'll go ahead and warn you—if they ask me what my involvement in this was, I'm going to blame it all on you and Luke."

I shrugged. "I know. It's what we decided on."

"All right," he said dubiously as he reached for the buttons on the door and rolled down the two passenger-side windows.

"Miss Lakely?" cried the face in the window. I stared back at the reporters. There weren't quite as many of them as I had first perceived—certainly not nearly as many as we had run into at the field house. I suspected that some of them were still in the stadium and some of them had probably gone home. Outside there stood only four.

The lady in the window was holding a microphone, and there was a man behind her with a video camera. Another man was still snapping pictures through the front window, and a gentleman behind him stood with his pencil poised over his pad, at the ready. "Are you Tricia Lakely?" the lady repeated.

"Um, yes, that's me," I replied as the cameraman moved behind the car to shoot through the back window.

"And Luke Benson, I presume?" she continued, looking past me to Luke.

"Yeah," he replied.

"Can I ask you a few questions?" I wondered what she would do if I said no, but she didn't wait for an answer. "What was your involvement in today's incident?"

When I didn't respond, she must have picked up on the fact that I was waiting for her to clarify a bit. I wasn't going to say anything until I found out exactly what she knew.

"It's been reported that there was some sort of chase in which Mr. Bobby Joe Fink was firing a gun at you and threatening Mr. Benson. And now, Mr. Fink is dead of a gunshot wound and Investigator Sam Buckson has reported that he has in his possession evidence which proves Mr. Fink was responsible for the death of Paul Sanders, the referee who was found dead after the recent Homecoming game here at Carrier High. Also, earlier this afternoon, a student, Aaron Tyler, was arrested for the crime. Now, after these new developments, Investigator Sam Buckson tells us that this young man has been released without being charged. What can you tell us about what happened?"

"Um, well, I sort of stumbled onto the final piece of evidence that the police were looking for." Yeah, they had been looking for it—they just didn't quite know it yet. "Bobby Joe Fink discovered that I had this piece of evidence in my possession, and he chased me here in his pickup. I turned onto the track, where he shot out my tire, and I escaped to the field house. My friend Luke, here, had been waiting for me in the parking lot, and Mr. Fink took him hostage to force me to give him the evidence. That's when Mr. Fink was shot."

"That's incredible," the lady said, her eyes widening a bit. The other reporter was scribbling away at that notepad for all he was worth. "And who shot Mr. Fink? Was it the police?"

"No, it wasn't the police. I'm not sure who it was. The shot came from the cliff, and I couldn't get a good look at the gunman. As far as I know, he's still unidentified."

"And this piece of evidence . . . could you tell me what it was, and how you came across it."

"Um, could you excuse me?" I replied, gratefully spotting a white Chevy Cavalier turning into the parking lot and pulling into the space beside Aaron's car. The face inside was Jackie Carrico's.

"Let's go, Joe," I said hastily.

He nodded and quickly fired up the engine. "I called her on my cell phone while you were asleep. She knows everything," Joe explained as he pulled up next to Jackie's car. "We really ought to try to keep the reporters off her back, you know," he said, gesturing to the four people trotting after us.

"Oh no," Luke groaned.

"What?" I asked, turning around to follow his gaze out the back window.

"Look at that," he replied. A whole swarm of people was pouring through the back gate and out of the stadium, headed our way.

"Come on," Joe said, opening his door and getting out. Luke and I also got out and followed Joe onto the grass.

Jackie got out of her car and came running to meet us. "I can't believe this!" she exclaimed as she reached us. "Tricia, Luke, are you guys all right?"

Luke nodded. "Yeah," I confirmed. "We're fine. Come on, though, we're going to try to keep the reporters off you."

The reporters were running after us, hot on our trail, which was a bit too short for my comfort, I might add. A police car with a familiar form in the backseat turned into the parking lot, made its way through the upper bus zone, and pulled alongside the sidewalk. Joe, Luke, Jackie, and I ran toward the car, knowing our wait was over.

The cop, who happened to be a young woman, got out of the car, walked around the front of her vehicle, and opened Aaron's door. Aaron climbed eagerly out. He had been able to take only one step forward when he found Jackie in his arms.

The policewoman shut the door. "You're sure you'll be all

right?" she asked Aaron.

"Yes. That's my car right over there," he replied, pointing to the little green car in the parking lot.

"All right," she nodded. "And good luck," she added with a raised eyebrow as the press rushed toward us. "I think I'm going to get out of here now." She headed for the driver's side, got in, and drove off, probably glad to leave the mob to us.

"Let's get out of here, shall we?" Aaron suggested mildly.

"What do you say we all meet at Pizza Hut?" Joe suggested softly. "Everyone go in different directions, and we'll try to throw them off."

The five of us walked briskly down the sidewalk toward the parking lot, ignoring the cries of the press who had been waiting for us on the lawn. They followed us and flowed into the parking lot. We were too quick for them, however, and we were all inside our cars before they had a chance to properly surround us. Luke and I were in the backseat of Joe's Mustang again, and Jackie had already backed out and driven away.

"Could you give us a ride over to my truck?" Luke asked.

"Sure," Joe replied. "Most of them will probably follow us since none but those four got an interview from you two. I doubt anyone much will follow Jackie, since they don't know who she is, and I'd think only those four, maybe, would follow Aaron." Joe backed out of his parking space, drove to the entrance by the stadium gate, and crossed.

As expected, the press poured across the road after us and into the stadium both by the main gate we had gone through, and the side one, directly in the middle of the back of the home stands. Joe drove around the track, back to the field house.

Luckily, even the fastest of the runners couldn't beat us there. Luke and I quickly climbed out of the car, jogged over to his truck, and got in.

Joe pulled up alongside us, and Luke rolled down his window. "Hey," Joe called to us. "Notice how all their vans are still over there?" He pointed to the section of the school parking lot filled with vans and cars—the reporters' transportation. "Let's wait a minute."

A minute was all it took for the stragglers to close the gap and come pouring around the track. Luke started his truck and pulled forward, almost seeming to be going to meet them. But he backed around in a paved space beside the end of the field house and turned to follow the empty track in the opposite direction.

We heard a shout from behind us as the reporters turned around to run back after us, but it was too late. By the time they made it back to the gate, we would have turned—and none of them would have seen which way we went. Luke hit the gas, paused at the gate to look, and then turned left and disappeared around the curve.

Joe was the last to arrive. "I thought I'd never get through that mess," he commented dryly as he sat down. After that, none of us really wanted to discuss the matter.

"So, what really happened?" Aaron asked. "All I know is that Sam Buckson is convinced that Bobby Joe is the killer, and that he's dead."

"I recognized the shirt," I began. "I have a picture of Paul at a birthday party he threw for me wearing the same gray sweatshirt that Bobby Joe wore after he murdered Paul. I was pretty upset about the whole thing, and you getting arrested and all, so I drove down to Bobby Joe's and got the shirt without thinking twice. He caught me leaving and chased me all the way back here, trying to shoot out my tires. I was circling the track when he shot out my tire and I ran in the field house."

"The field house? What time was it?"

"I don't know. Maybe ten minutes after school let out. It didn't take me long at the apartment."

"But how did you . . . I mean the guys would have been—"

"Changing?" I sighed. "Yes, I know." Aaron stared at me. "Oh, shut up Aaron."

"I didn't say anything," he protested, trying not to smile.

"Anyway, that's where I came in," Luke took over. "I was waiting for Tricia in the parking lot, and when I saw her on the track with Bobby Joe after her, I ran across the road. Only trouble was, by the time I got there, Tricia was already inside, and Bobby Joe decided to grab me and put a gun to my head." Luke shuddered. "Not fun. He hollered that if Tricia didn't come out, he'd shoot me. And I, for one, believed him. At any rate Tricia came out, the cops got there, and he got shot."

"By the cops?" Aaron asked quickly.

"No," I replied. "That's just it. He offered to tell me who hired him, and then some gunman dressed in black shot him from the top of the cliff behind the stadium. I have no idea who he was, and apparently neither did the cops."

"Odd," Aaron said quietly. "So Buckson's got all the evidence now?"

"Yeah. And I'm glad. He strictly told us to keep our noses out of it from here on out and let them find this other guy, but—"

"But I know you," Aaron grinned.

"But," Joe broke in, "we decided that you and I shouldn't actively be involved at this point. The killer doesn't necessarily know we're in on it, and we've got Coach Jones and everyone else watching us. Tricia and Luke will keep us informed, but they're going to have to keep a low profile, too. I'm afraid that this is going to be about the last full-fledged conspiracy meeting."

Aaron smiled. "Well, I suppose I'll rather miss it."

"Me too," Joe agreed.

There was an awkward silence after that which none of the four of us were quite willing to break—that left it up to Jackie. "So what happened to you, Aaron?" she asked after a moment.

"After they searched my car and found the bag that Fink had planted there, they arrested me, read me my rights, put me in the police car, and took me off to the police station. They finger-printed me and all that, and then lucky me got to sit in one of about three cells in the place by myself, wishing I at least had a deck of cards to play solitaire. It was pretty boring."

"I'll bet," Joe mumbled.

I glanced down at my watch. "Merciful heavens," I blurted. Four faces looked up at me sharply. "It's past five o' clock!"

"Will your mother be expecting you home?" Aaron asked, confused.

"Not only that, but she's at home with the five o'clock news on, no doubt!"

"And I'll bet I know what the top story is," Luke groaned.

"I'm sorry," I apologized, "but I've got to go."

"I'll give you a ride," Luke offered.

"Thanks," I replied gratefully. "We'll keep you guys posted," I promised.

CHAPTER SIXTEEN

"I suppose it's a good thing for me that my mom never watches local news and isn't a really big radio fan, either," Luke commented as he pulled into my driveway. "Do you think she'll be upset?"

"I don't know," I sighed. "She doesn't deal with this stuff very well. Especially not after Dad died." I opened the door and stepped out. "Thanks for bringing me home, Luke."

"No problem," he replied.

I was walking around the front of the truck when Luke opened his own door and quickly got out of the truck. I looked at him questioningly.

"Look," he said, "maybe I ought to walk you in."

"You really don't have to do that," I protested.

"No, I want to," he insisted.

I shrugged. "All right then." We walked side by side up the concrete walk, and I softly pulled the door open, not quite knowing what to expect inside.

My first instinct was to shut the door, turn around, and walk away, but that certainly wouldn't have helped matters any. Besides, to some degree, this was my own fault. There I was, on TV, telling the lady with the microphone what had happened. I hadn't gotten a good enough look at the camera to tell which station it was from—naturally, it had to be this one.

Mom was sobbing her eyes out on the couch. Francis Whitman was sitting beside her, muttering something about how he was sure I was all right and looking completely at a loss for what to do. He spotted me first—Mom hadn't heard me open the door.

"Uh, Amy. . . ," he mumbled.

Mom looked up, took one look at me, and jumped to her feet. "Tricia!" she gasped, darting over to the doorway where Luke and I stood. She grabbed my hand as if to be sure that I was really there. "Are you all right?"

"I'm fine," I replied slowly, wondering frantically how I was going to explain all this.

"You're not hurt?"

"No. I'm fine."

"What is all this?" she demanded, pointing at the television. "Is all this true? Was that man shooting at you?"

"Well, he wasn't exactly shooting at *me*, Mom," I said as soothingly as I could manage. "He just shot out my tire was all."

"Why was he shooting at you?"

I shrugged. "I had something he wanted. He killed Paul Sanders back at the Homecoming game, and I just happened to have the last piece of evidence needed to incriminate him."

"Happened to have? Tricia where did you get it?"

I stared at the floor. I couldn't tell her. She'd have a heart attack and die or something horrible like that. Mom hated surprises. "Look Mom, it doesn't matter. I found it, I knew what it was, and I fully intended to give it to the police. I wanted to find Paul's killer, and I did."

"You mean this was all you?"

"What was all me?"

"You said the *last* piece of evidence. Were you connected in any way to any of the others?"

I shifted uneasily. To say *no* would be an outright lie. . . . "Yes."

"How much of it?"

I sighed. "Just about all of it."

Mom stared at me incredulously. "You'd better start explaining, young lady."

"Look, Mom. When Paul died and Aaron was the prime suspect, I decided that I wanted to find the real killer, first so Paul could rest in peace because he was my friend, and second because I know Aaron, and I knew he wasn't a murderer. So I got some help, and we solved the murder. That's it. Sam Buckson told us not to tell the press because whoever killed Bobby Joe Fink is still out there, and we think he's the one who hired Fink to kill Paul in the first place. So we're supposed to stay out of the rest of the investigation, and we aren't supposed to tell the press anything much for our own safety. And so Sam Buckson and the police department can keep the credit for solving the murder, if you ask me."

"Darn right you're going to stay out of it!" Mom exclaimed. "I can't believe you were foolish enough to get caught up in something like this in the first place! Don't you have any sense at all?

"And you," she continued, turning to Luke. "Who are you?"

"Hello, Mrs. Lakely," Luke said awkwardly, a bit surprised. "I—"

"Oh, I remember you," she cut him off. "Luke. You're that Benson character, aren't you? Yes, that's you. Luke Benson, right?"

"Yes, ma'am. That's me."

"And what are you, her partner in crime?"

"Well, I—"

"Don't bother trying to explain. And which one of you started all this?"

"I did," I replied.

"Well not anymore," Mom snapped. "This partnership is officially over. You, young lady, are going to stay out of trouble, and if that means not seeing Mr. Luke Benson, then so be it."

My eyes widened. "But Mom, it's not his fault!"

"That's enough!" Mom shouted. I was afraid she was about to collapse. I'd never seen her like this, and frankly, she was beginning to scare me. "You will never, ever engage in this recklessness ever again, do you understand me? Have you got any idea what I would do if anything happened to you? Any idea at all?"

I stared at her, not knowing what to say.

"Mrs. Lakely, please—" Luke tried again.

Mom turned on him, her eyes flashing. "You just get on home, young man," she said a bit more calmly. At least she wasn't yelling anymore, but her words seemed to be having the same effect on Luke as if she had been still screaming. "I may never know what went on between you two and what your part in all this was. But I do know you had one. And I do know Tricia. And I know that she's not one to give up easily. So that's it. I'm not taking a chance on you two getting buried in this. Don't bother asking to take my daughter out again for a long time, because the answer's going to be *no.* As long as I can't trust you or her, she's not to see you outside of school. Is that understood?"

"Mother!" I gasped. She couldn't do that to me!

"Is that understood?" She was yelling again.

Apparently, this was all Luke could take. "Yes, ma'am." He turned to go. "For what it's worth, ma'am, I'm sorry that it ended like this. It wasn't what we had planned." With that he walked down the concrete walk to his truck, and Mom slammed the door behind him.

I stared at her dumbly, not quite knowing what to say.

"Oh, Tricia," she sobbed, fresh tears pouring from her eyes. "You know I couldn't bear to lose you." With that, she put her arms around my shoulders and held me close, as if she feared someone would take me away.

"I'm sorry, Mom," I mumbled. "I was just trying to do what's right."

"I know," she sighed. Finally, she let go of me, and her eyes widened. "I had no right to speak to that young man like that, did I?" she said softly. She ran to the door and pulled it open, but Luke was already gone. "How horrible of me," she said, coming back inside. "After the two of you have had such a hard day and all."

"Oh, Mom, I'm sure he understood," I promised with more surety than I felt. "Luke's a very understanding person."

"But I bit his head off—"

"Mom." I looked her straight in the eye. "What's done is done, and fretting about it isn't going to change things. I'll get it all patched up tomorrow. Look, I'm sorry about all of this. I never meant to betray your trust. This was just something I had to do, and, if anything, I'm the one who dragged Luke into it."

"All right," she sighed. "What's done is done. Tell him I am sorry, and that I'm not upset with him. And I'm not upset with you, Tricia. You just scared me, that's all. And I don't like to be scared."

"I noticed." My eyes narrowed. "So does that mean that you take it back? I mean, about not seeing Luke?"

"Can you promise me that the two of you won't so much as discuss anything pertaining to this case?"

I shifted from foot to foot. I couldn't straight-out lie to my own mother! Especially if I expected to get away with it. I was far too transparent for that—Mom and I had known each other a long time.

"That's what I thought. Look, I have nothing against this boy. I'm sure he's a very nice, brave young man. But I really do want you to stay out of this, Tricia. I mean it. Until you can make that promise and not break it, I'm not going to permit you to go out with him."

There was no arguing with her. "All right," I sighed.

After a few more hugs and about a thousand apologies to Francis from both of us for the scene, we finally sat down to dinner. As I picked at my lemon pepper chicken, I wondered what would have happened if Francis hadn't been there when Mom found out. True, he hadn't known what to do, but being there had been enough. In fact, if it weren't for Francis's sudden appearance, I might not have been able to slip past her to solve the case at all. Fortunately for me, her mind was otherwise occupied, and she hadn't really wondered much about what I was up to. It was true that I wasn't really all that impressed with Francis, but he may have been what Mom needed right now.

Walking into Carrier High the next day was like stepping into a whole different world. I guess I should have expected the awed stares and the sixteen million questions, but I hadn't ever really stopped to think about it. I patiently repeated the same thing I had told the reporters, refusing to say anything else and insisting that I just happened upon this piece of evidence.

I suspected that most everybody knew the truth, anyway. Rachael had told me that everyone suspected that Luke, Aaron, Joe, and I were up to something of this sort, and their knowing smiles when I clamped my mouth shut seemed to confirm that. All in all, it was pretty unsettling.

Everything was worth it, though, when I saw Aaron slip back into his normal spot in high school life, getting an unusual number of pats on the back and shameful apologies. At least Aaron had learned something from this experience—who his true friends were. Jackie was beaming. She was happier than I had seen her in a long time—since all of this began, anyway. It was over for her, and she and Aaron had won.

I certainly hoped Aaron appreciated her—most normal girls would have dumped him on the spot. But Jackie had stood by him through it all, and I knew that he was grateful.

Luke didn't seem quite himself. That was expected, considering what we had been through yesterday, but I was still worried about him. He seemed to lighten up a bit when I explained how Mom had just been upset and hadn't meant anything that she said. It probably helped for him to know that she was sorry about it. He still wasn't happy about the fact that she still wasn't going to let us get together out of school, though.

"What are we going to do?" Luke asked as we sat with our desks together in Spanish class. We were supposed to be translating another lesson. Yeah, right. "How are we supposed to piece this together if we can't work together?"

"I think that's the point," I replied.

"Yeah, well, we're not giving up, are we?"

I sighed. "I'm not into the teen rebellion thing, but no. I'm not going to give up. I just hope that she'll understand. If something isn't done soon, and the killer gets suspicious, you and I could be in danger. We're at risk until he's brought in."

"I wish the game was home tomorrow," Luke said. "Then we could work there. But it's at Fredericksville."

I shrugged. "I don't know. I have the list Joe copied, but I'm going to let you have it. The last thing I want is for it to fall into the hands of my mother." I pulled the papers out of my book bag and handed them to him. "You look them over first and see if anything looks interesting. For now that's all that we can do."

"Yeah, I guess so." Luke slipped the papers into his own book bag. "Maybe we'll be able to come up with some way to work together. It'll be hard to do it apart like this."

"I know. But hey, look at it this way—there *is* something we can do right now," I said.

"What's that?"

I pointed to my book. "Translate this."

Luke sighed.

Luke and I were walking down the hall after Spanish class when we were intercepted by Rachael Blair. "Tricia!" she exclaimed. "I'm so proud of you two! I'm glad you didn't get hurt."

"Yeah, me too," I laughed.

"How did your mom take it?" Rachael asked seriously.

"Not too well, but she's all right now."

"She didn't ground you or anything, did she?"

"No, not specifically."

"Are you still going to be able to come over to study tomorrow night?"

"Oh yeah. I'd almost forgotten. Yeah, Mom said I could go before. Shouldn't be a problem."

Rachael gave me an odd look. "You mean she didn't restrict your movements at all?"

"Well. . . ."

"Well, what?"

"She said I can't see Luke outside of school until this is all resolved."

Rachael whistled. "She's trying to make you stay out of it,

isn't she?"

"Yeah. But she doesn't understand that we're at risk until he's caught, and we could help."

"But now we can't work together anymore," Luke concluded.

"Exactly," I sighed.

"Well," Rachael said, her smile widening, "if you two want to be together that much. . . ."

"What are you getting at, Rachael?" I asked carefully.

"Luke, would you like to come over to my house tomorrow to study for Burton's big test with Tricia and me?"

Luke raised an eyebrow. "I don't have Burton this semester."

Rachael winked. "So?"

Friday found me in my truck again, coasting down Horizon Drive on a brand new front tire with the little tape containing Sam Buckson's conversation nestled in my pocket. All day Thursday I'd had a tugging feeling that I had forgotten something, and lying in bed that night I remembered what it was.

Back on the first day, when we had searched Paul's house, we found a little slip of paper with "286AHD" under a magnet on the refrigerator. We'd been at this for nearly three weeks now, and we had never come across that number again. I remembered that Sam Buckson had mentioned it in his conversation, but I couldn't remember exactly what he had said. Since I didn't have a miniature tape player, and Rachael obviously did, I was bringing it along to find out exactly what he had said.

I turned onto Anchor Head Drive and drove for a few miles, each curve seeming to fade into the next. I took a right onto the gravel drive that was, by now, quite familiar. It wound back on a track sandwiched between a steep hill covered with trees and vegetation and the gurgling brook that skipped over stones in the streambed, parallel to the road. Finally the hill folded back and the stream crossed under a small bridge to rim its bottom on the other side. Wooden fences picked up on both sides of the drive where the stream and trees had left off, to run alongside the driveway, almost up to the house.

The house itself was a split foyer, part brick, and part a lovely cream colored siding. It was a charming thing, planted right here in the middle of this little valley that most people would never see. Yes, Rachael was a farm girl. But I certainly envied her in that she had the best view in Judsonville—at least the best I'd seen—and a pretty buckskin quarter horse named Cody.

This was the sort of place that no matter how many times you visit it, you always want to come back. I felt that way, anyway. And apparently so did a lot of other people—Rachael's house was never empty.

There was almost always someone with a last name other than *Blair* there, usually one or more friends of Rachael's younger brother, Justin. There were probably times when it seemed like this one house was supporting about half of Carrier High's male sophomore population. It certainly was a popular place.

Rachael's mom greeted me at the door with the same cheerful smile she always wore. In fact, I couldn't remember ever seeing her without it. I could hear several male voices downstairs—it was a full house tonight, as always. I made my way down the hall on the upper level to Rachael's room, the last door on the right. There she was, stretched out on her bed with Celine Dion's voice pouring out of the nearby stereo.

"Hey there, Tricia!" Rachael greeted me, sitting up and gesturing for me to have a seat on the bed beside her. "Just chilling out for a while."

"Sounded like your brother's got friends over."

Rachael grinned. "As always. Jake and Peter, this time."

"Jake Hall?"

"Yeah. Melissa's little brother. And Peter Smith."

"Don't know him."

"Kinda tall and lean, red hair, not bad looking, plays basketball. . . ."

I nodded. "Yeah. I think I know who you're talking about. Sophomore, right?"

"Yeah. Aren't they all?"

I shrugged. "Do you suppose Luke will find his way down here all right?"

"Suppose I'll manage," Luke replied as he walked through the door. "I do have to admit that I was starting to think I was lost, though. Quite a place you have here." He sat down. "Your mom was really friendly." Luke looked at Rachael uncertainly. "Are you sure she doesn't mind my just showing up?"

Rachael and I shared a knowing smile. "Nah," Rachael laughed as she leaned over to turn off her stereo. "As long as she doesn't have to feed you, she doesn't care at all. Heck, we host a bunch of Justin's friends every weekend. Probably about three quarters of the sophomore class have had a meal here before."

"Gee." I suspected that Luke's family life was a more normal one than Rachael and I had ever experienced. He didn't quite understand the workings of Rachael's house, but after tonight I was sure he'd fit in just fine— just like the other forty percent of Carrier High that "lived" here.

"Well," Rachael prompted, "shall we?"

I sighed. "If we must."

"But I thought you wanted to look over this stuff with him," Rachel said. "Wasn't that the whole point?"

"I figured you'd want to study first."

Rachael laughed. "Study? How much studying did you actually expect us to get done, Tricia?"

"Just enough to get by." I grinned.

"And you and I both know that's not much," she agreed. "Besides, I can study all weekend. Right now I'm curious as to know what's going on."

Luke pulled the folded papers out of his pocket. He unfolded the list and handed it to me, sitting down on the bed beside me. "Do you remember that number we found at Paul's house, that *286AHD?*" he asked. "Well, since this is Paul's delivery list from Venny's for that Friday, I checked it to see if that might apply to any of the addresses. It matched up to only one—286 Anchor Head Drive."

"Whoa, wait a sec," Rachael interrupted. "That's my address! You're sitting in 286 Anchor Head Drive!"

"Hmm," I muttered. "Rachael, did you have a delivery from Venny's on that Friday?"

"Let me think. . . ." Rachael straightened up. "Yeah. I remember now. Justin got a Nintendo game from Larry's shop. It was back ordered, and he'd been waiting for it for months. So, naturally, he invited over about six of his buddies to try it out the next day."

"Well, X that one off," I sighed. "No other matches?"

"Nope. The only other roads that I could think of that would even come close would be Hickory or Horizon. There aren't any deliveries on Hickory, but there's a couple on Horizon. There's a 285 Horizon Drive, but that's got a *five* instead of a *six*, and it leaves out the *A* altogether."

"Wait, wait!" This time it was me who interrupted. "That can't be right! That's *my* address, and I know we didn't get any deliveries from Venny's lately." I creased my eyebrows. "But—if memory serves, the guy across the street had just moved in, and we got one of his packages, and Mom had to send the delivery guy across the street. She told me about it. But she doesn't know Paul, so nothing about it really stuck in my memory that well. Still, I think it was for Francis."

"Francis?" Rachael asked incredulously. "The gorgeous guy's name is Francis?"

I nodded. "Francis Whitman. Mom calls him Frank."

"What's his address?" Luke asked quickly.

My eyes narrowed, taking me back to the day that I had seen him put up his mailbox. Had it been. . . . My eyes widened rapidly again. "Yes! That was it!" I said triumphantly. "286-A Horizon Drive. There's a trailer right beside the property, but closer to the road. It was there first, so it was 286. And then when the log house got put in, they must have added an A."

"So now the big question is what does it mean?" Luke asked.

I shrugged. "I don't know."

"Paul didn't say anything about it the night he was killed?"

I tried to remember. "He said he had a stop to make after the game," I replied slowly. "And then he said he would see me tomorrow—" I paused, trying to clear the breath that caught in my throat. "If he wasn't dead." I took a deep breath. Those words would haunt me for the rest of my life. "I can't remember what Sam Buckson said about those numbers, so let's put this back in," I suggested, pulling the tiny cassette tape out of my pocket.

Rachael reached down into the book bag on the floor, propped against the bed, and pulled out her mini tape recorder. I handed her the tape, and she popped it in. She pushed PLAY, and we heard . . . nothing.

"Hmm," Rachael muttered, moving the volume dial. Finally she looked up at me and asked suspiciously, "Did you rewind it?"

"Ah. . . ," I replied guiltily, "no."

"Tricia, Tricia," Rachael scolded, stopping the tape, and popping the recorder door open. She pulled the tape out, flipped it over, shoved it back in, and hit FAST FORWARD. "That's the only thing I have against this thing," she commented. "It hasn't got a rewind. You have to do an awful lot of tape flipping if you miss something."

She pressed STOP and was about to pull out the tape, but her hand stopped in midair. "I wonder if I recorded anything on this tape before I gave it to you?" she said out loud. "I'm missing one of Burton's lectures on the first quiz in this chapter. I'm gonna check and see if this is it." With that, she pressed PLAY.

The voice that came from the tape recorder was definitely not Burton's. It took me a few moments to realize who it was, and when I figured it out, I about jumped out of my skin.

"Who's that?" Luke asked curiously.

"Not a clue," Rachael replied in an odd tone of voice.

"That's Francis Whitman," I gasped.

Rachael stopped the tape. "New guy?"

"Yeah."

Rachael stared at me. "You mean new guy who lives at 286-A Horizon Drive and's dating your mom?"

"Yeah. Rachael, where did you get that tape?"

"Wait!" Rachael exclaimed. "Remember when you called me and I told you that new guy was stranded so I got him some gas and took his trash? Well, when the bag broke, a lot of stuff fell out. Most of it was boxes and stuff, probably from moving. But this tape fell out, and I figured it just got thrown out by mistake with a bunch of other stuff. So, remember how I said I'm always running out of these things? Why throw one away if it isn't busted?"

"Rachael! You just picked that thing up out of Francis Whitman's trash and took it?"

"Why not?" she answered defensively. "He wasn't using it."

I laughed. "Oh well. Let's take it back to the beginning and see what he was babbling about. Sam Buckson can wait."

Rachael obediently took the tape out, turned it over, and fast forwarded it to the end. Then she quickly took it out and put it back in on the other side again.

The buzz of the tape recorder was eerie in the few moments of complete silence before Francis Whitman's voice came on. "Hi. You've reached 555-7659. Leave a message at the tone."

"Short and sweet," I noted.

"Hey, Frankie boy," came an unfamiliar voice. "Look, I know you're there. Do me a favor and pick up. Look, Frankie, I don't have all day. . . ."

"Sorry, Scottie," Francis's voice came on. "I was a little busy."

"Doing what?" Scottie demanded tensely.

"Having a little quality time in the privacy of my own bathroom if it's all right with you."

I blinked. This was certainly a different Francis than the charming "Frank" who spent most of his time trying to impress my mother.

"Sorry, Frankie, but I'm getting a little nervous here."

"Don't wet your pants, Scotty, I just got it."

"You did?"

"Yup. Not a bad move using that Venny's shipping thing. It'll be harder to trace than if you'd used UPS or something like that. Although I must say it would've helped if you'd used the right address—you were a number off, and you're lucky I got this."

"Yeah, well, punch me next time you see me, if it makes you happy. You hit like a girl anyway. Have you opened it yet?"

"Just glanced. I only got it about two minutes ago, and then nature called."

"Whatever. Just count it, okay?"

"Yeah, yeah. Give me a sec."

There was a pause. I didn't even realize that I was holding my breath until the heat rose warningly to my cheeks. I took a quick gasp as Francis's voice came back on. "All here. All five hundred thousand of it. A nice, pretty, half a million. So what happened? All I got was the brief news-report version."

"I don't know exactly what happened. We'd just made the deal, and the cops showed. I split, and so did Frazier. He got caught, I didn't. Simple as that. Frazier's pretty PO'd, though. I eliminated the first incompetent he sent for me, but the next one might be worse. For now, I'm gonna lie low. I'm hiding out in a rat hole in Roanoke, and as soon as things quiet down, I'm headed for Nashville."

"If I were you, I'd go clear to LA."

"Naw. Them California dogs are pretty rough. I'd rather take my chances in Nashville, thanks. At any rate, they can't get anything solid on me as long as you've got the money. Just do me a favor, Frankie—don't get caught." There was a pause, and then the voice returned with an irritated tone. "What's that noise, Frankie?"

"Noise?"

"That buzz! It's about to drive me nuts."

Francis swore. I blinked. If Mom ever heard him talk like that, she would slap his face—hard. "I left the machine on. Hold on a sec, and I'll cut it off."

"Don't bother now—it's too late. You'll have to destroy the tape and get a new one."

Francis muttered a few choice profanities under his breath. There was another pause followed by a surprised shout.

"What's going on, Frankie?" Scotty asked skittishly.

"That deliveryman is hanging around my front window! He's running now, but I think he saw the money! Hold on!" I heard the pounding of feet. After a few moments, Francis's voice returned. "He got away. He must have been onto me."

"Do you know who he was?"

"Said his name was Paul—what, I don't know. But he was talking about refereeing a game tonight—Judsonville Mustangs he said. That's the local high school. It's their Homecoming. I'll find out who he is."

"When you do, eliminate him. I don't want any chances here. I'm hangin' out in the open here, and I don't like it. I'd really like to make it to Nashville, you know."

"I'll stash the money, get rid of this referee loser, and you get out of Dodge, you hear?"

"Roanoke."

"Whatever. You're not gonna make it much longer if Frazier's on your tail."

"I'll contact you later. Don't try to get me unless it's an emergency, and I mean a pretty serious one. In that case ring up Carla. She'll know where I am."

"All right. Play it safe, partner."

"You too. And get rid of this tape will ya?"

"No prob."

"And get rid of Snoopy tonight. Don't do him yourself—it's too risky right now, and I can't have you getting caught. If memory serves, there's a Roscoe Thompson down there, pretty respectable and all, as far as loan sharks go. Haven't managed to tick him off yet, so if you give him a bit of a tip, he should be able to give you a name. Stay out of trouble, you hear? Hope Snoopy has a nice funeral." He chuckled. I wanted to deck him.

"Yeah. I'll take care of it."

"Bye, Frankie."

"Bye, Scotty."

There was a click and then silence.

"Dear God," I whispered. I stared at the ceiling. "Oh help me, God," I prayed fervently. "Tell me this isn't happening."

CHAPTER SEVENTEEN

I drove home in a daze. I could remember that afternoon a few weeks ago so clearly. . . . I had been driving home in my truck, listening to the radio report of the drug bust in Roanoke. I remembered thinking that nothing exciting ever happened here in Judsonville. How could I have been so wrong? How could I know that the very same case would carry over into my own life?

Luke had insisted on coming along, probably afraid I would do something rash in regard to Francis Whitman. He knew as well as I did that Francis would probably be there when I got home. I had patiently reminded Luke that he was forbidden to see me outside of school, but he insisted that he would park next door and just wait to see if there was trouble. I had to admit that it was better to be safe than sorry. Francis was capable of more than I had ever imagined giving him credit for—a lot more.

All the lights were off in the Casey residence, next door. Old Mr. and Mrs. Casey went to bed pretty early—both of them were always up with the sun. On lazy spring Saturday mornings, no matter how early I managed to drag myself out of bed, I could always look out the window and see Mrs. Casey already busy at work in her flower bed. At any rate, there didn't seem to be any activity in the house as Luke turned his lights off and turned into their drive.

I pulled up in front of the garage, turned off my lights, and cut off the engine. I sat still for a moment, taking deep breaths, and then I unbuckled my seat belt, opened the door, and resolutely stepped out of my faithful old truck. I made my way to the front door, walking with an air of confidence that I didn't really feel. Hoping I could trick myself into being brave, I raised my chin a bit as I pulled open the front door and stepped casually inside.

As I had expected, Mom sat on the couch watching television,

Francis Whitman's arm around her shoulders. Just for that, I could have broken his nose on the spot. But instead I gritted my teeth and strolled into the living room as if nothing were wrong. "Hey, Mom," I smiled. "Hi, Francis."

"Hi, sweetheart," Mom replied. "You didn't stay too long."

"Nah. It's not a real hard test. Rachael had some other stuff to do, so I just came on home. Thought I'd get some extra sleep tonight."

"Good idea," Francis laughed. "I remember when I was a teenager, I never seemed to be able to get enough sleep." Mom smiled at him and squeezed his hand.

I resisted another urge to take a swing at Francis. I had to put a stop to this. "Mom, I need to talk to you about something," I said.

"What is it, sweetheart?"

"Could I talk to you alone?" I asked a bit apologetically. "I know you're busy, but it's kind of important."

Mom raised an eyebrow. "Does this have anything to do with males?" she asked, as if she already knew.

"Well, you could say that, I guess," I said, trying to look uncomfortable for Francis's benefit.

It seemed to work. He nodded knowingly. "You'd better go, Amy," he suggested. "These things can get pretty serious."

"Tell me about it," I muttered. "Thanks, Francis," I beamed. "Hopefully this won't take too long. I'll have her back before you know it." I winked at him and led Mom down the hall to her bedroom. She followed me in and shut the door behind her.

"What is it, sweetheart?" she asked again as I sat down on the bed.

"You'd better sit down, Mom," I warned. She gave me an odd look but sat down beside me. "Look, I don't know where to start. This is pretty complicated. Do you remember when you told me not to see Luke outside of school?"

"Is that what this is about, Tricia?" she asked. "You have a crush on him, don't you, sweetie? And you want me to let you date him."

"Well, that's not exactly it, Mom."

"Then what is it?"

"Look, Mom, try not to be too mad, okay?"

"You already saw him, didn't you?" she guessed. "Tonight?"

I nodded.

"You lied about going to Rachael's?" she demanded.

"No. I was at Rachael's, and I didn't go anywhere else. Luke just happened to show up while I was over there. I didn't lie, Mom."

She sighed. "No, I guess not."

"Mom, something happened while we were over at Rachael's studying. Rachael records all of Burton's important lectures on a mini tape recorder to help her study. Now, she never seems to have enough of those little tapes, so when she found one in good shape one day, she kept it, you know, thinking she could still get good use out of it.

"It just so happened that one day Francis"—I nodded my head toward the door—"was broken down on the side of the road, out of gas. Since he was on his way to take his trash to the Dumpsters, she got him some gas and took his trash for him, wanting to be a good neighbor and all. Well, the trash bag broke while she was getting it out of the car, and this tape fell out along with some boxes and stuff. Like I said, she kept it, and threw the rest away.

"We had just listened to a tape and Rachael was checking to see if a lecture she lost was by any chance on the other side.We got a recorded phone conversation instead. That tape had come out of Francis's answering machine."

"You didn't listen to it, did you?" she asked, horrified at our bad manners.

"Of course we listened to it. And it's a good thing we did. Francis had forgotten to turn off his machine, so we had the entire conversation. You're not going to believe this, Mom."

"What?" she asked flatly, probably about to lose patience with me.

I took a deep breath. In a low voice, I said, "Mom, Francis Whitman is the one who hired Bobby Joe Fink to kill Paul Sanders."

She stared at me. "Of all the stupid—Tricia, how could you make something like that up?"

"We didn't make it up, Mom! It's all plain and clear on the tape."

"You must be reading things into it."

"No, Mom. Francis is into drugs, and his partner got into some trouble during a deal in Roanoke. The buyer got caught with the drugs, but Francis's partner got away and sent him the money through Venny's Shipping Company. Paul was the delivery guy, and he saw him open up the box with all the cash in it, and Francis had him killed, afraid he'd go to the police. Paul had said something about having to make a stop on his way home from the game. I'll bet that was where he was going."

Mom stared at me, unwilling to grasp the reality of the situation.

"This isn't speculation, Mom. This is real, and it's all on the tape. Luke's waiting outside in the Caseys' drive. I think you need to get rid of 'Frank,' invite Luke in, and we need to call the police. If we do this now, it can all be settled. Over. And then you won't have to forbid me from dating Luke, now will you?"

"How can you expect me to believe all this, Tricia?" Mom asked, her eyes a mystery. "Francis is a wonderful person. He's kind, and gentle—he doesn't even curse, for heaven's sake! He couldn't have someone killed!"

"But he did. And he killed Bobby Joe Fink himself. Plus, he does swear—a lot—if you listen to that tape. He even took the Lord's name in vain."

Her eyes flashed. "He did?" Remember what I said about Mom and swearing. . . .

"Yup. He's a real loser, Mom. Get rid of him before he hurts you—I mean physically. Just think up some reason why you need him to leave. You don't have to break up with him or anything, just politely say good night. Wait to tell him what a greasebag he is until he's in handcuffs, okay?"

She nodded slowly. Don't get me wrong—Mom is by no means a dense person. But if someone waltzed up and told you that your new boyfriend, who had so far proven to be perfect, was a murderer, what would you do? All in all, I thought she was handling it pretty well. Some people would already be fishing through their kitchen drawers for butcher knives.

"Okay," Mom said, gathering her thoughts. "I'll tell him I need some time alone with you and invite him over to dinner tomorrow to make him think everything's normal. I'll just tell him that it's one of those mother-daughter things. That ought to get him off our backs. Besides, he won't be keeping that dinner date if he's locked up in a cell somewhere." She gave me a penetrating look. "You're absolutely, without a doubt, positive that you're right about this?"

"Yes," I replied firmly. "Positive."

"All right then," she sighed, obviously fighting very hard to keep her emotions in check. I couldn't even imagine how that kind of betrayal must feel. To tell the truth, I didn't want to imagine it. "Let's go. Try to look a little upset," she instructed. "Not overly, just enough."

I nodded, and we marched bravely out of the room and back to the living room. I waited at the end of the hall to let her say good-bye to Francis alone. My fingers were crossed so tightly that it felt like blood would never circulate in them again.

Francis nodded understandingly as Mom explained the whole "mother-daughter thing" situation. As I watched him, I wondered if he really loved her. The thought was like jabbing a needle into my own stomach, but I had to acknowledge the possibility. In that moment, I had more respect for my mother than ever as she stood straight and smiled in the face of a man she probably hated right now.

Francis smiled and left with the promise of dinner tomorrow night. Mom closed the front door behind him and watched him cross the street to his own house and let himself in. Without another word she walked over to the couch and collapsed.

"Are you all right, Mom?"

"I'll be fine," she promised wearily. "Just go out there and get Luke so we can do this before my emotions have a chance to catch up with me."

"All right," I replied with more surety than I felt. I made my way out the back door. The stars glittered brightly in the dark night. I looked up at them, hoping for some sign that I was going to make it through tonight without getting myself, Mom, Luke, or any unlucky cops killed. I knew I was playing a dangerous game. I picked out a twinkling little star in some constellation I couldn't name, closed my eyes, and made a wish.

I walked around the corner of the house. As I stood in the shadow, I could get a clear view of Luke sitting in his parked truck, staring out the windshield at the same stars that I had just wished upon. I took two steps away from the house and out of the shadows. He caught sight of me, and I motioned for him to come here. He quickly got out of his truck and shut the door as quietly as possible. He made his way into the shadows beside my house and we headed back inside together.

Mom was waiting for us. "What should I do?" she asked, the

nervousness beginning to eat its way through and starting to show in her eyes. "Should I dial 911?"

"No," Luke said. "The sirens would alert him. We need to get ahold of Sam Buckson."

"I don't have his number," I replied, shaking my head.

"Wait a second," Luke said, taking a step forward. "You *do* have Melissa Hall's number."

"Good idea," I agreed, grabbing the cordless phone from the counter and punching in Melissa's number.

I waited impatiently as it rang. *Pick up*, I thought nervously.

"Hello?"

"Hi. Melissa?"

"Yeah. Tricia?"

"Look, Melissa. Could you put your dad on the phone?"

"My dad? Tricia, is something wrong?"

"Look, Melissa, I don't have time to explain. Please, put your dad on the phone."

"All right, all right. Hold on just a sec." I walked in circles, wishing he'd hurry up.

"Yes?" came the deep voice of Tommy Hall.

"Hi, Mr. Hall. This is Tricia Lakely. I'm the girl who gave you guys all that evidence about Bobby Joe Fink and the Paul Sanders murder."

"Yes?"

"Look, we came across something else by accident. I promise we haven't been doing any breaking and entering or anything like that this time. I need to get ahold of Sam Buckson. Can you give me his number?"

"Look, Tricia, we can't act on every hunch you kids come up with—"

"This isn't a hunch, Mr. Hall. This is solid evidence. Look, please just give me Sam Buckson's number. If this guy isn't brought in really soon, like tonight, my mom and I could be in danger. Please, just trust me and give me the number. The other evidence was legit, wasn't it?"

"Well, yes. . . ."

"Please, Mr. Hall. I beg you."

"All right, all right. You got paper and pencil?"

"Yeah, yeah," I replied, grabbing a pen out of a nearby basket and sliding the notepad closer to the edge of the counter. I scribbled down the number as Tommy Hall read it off to me.

"Thanks a lot, Mr. Hall," I said gratefully. "You might as well be ready. Sam's probably gonna call you back in a few minutes." With that I punched the red "end" button and quickly put in Sam's number. I turned and leaned against the counter as it rang, my toe beating against the floor over and over again.

"Hello?"

"Sam Buckson?"

"Investigator Sam Buckson here, can I help you?"

"Yeah. This is Tricia Lakely."

"What do you want?" he sighed.

"Look, we haven't been digging around, we just stumbled across this by accident, I swear. We know who hired Bobby Joe Fink and why."

"Start talking," he said cautiously.

"Okay. My friend Rachael ran into this guy one day who was broken down on the side of the road. So she got him some gas and took his trash for him, you know, just being neighborly. Well, the bag broke getting it out of the car, and she threw all the stuff out, but she picked up a little mini tape that was in the trash and kept it because she uses one of those mini tape recorders to record lectures in one of her classes.

"Anyway, I was studying at Rachael's house tonight, and when we'd finished with the first tape we listened to, we tried the other side to see if it was a lecture she couldn't locate, and we came across a phone conversation where the tape had been in this guy's answering machine."

"How do you know it was the same guy whose trash she took?"

"Because, he's my next-door neighbor and my mom's boyfriend," I replied matter-of-factly. "I know his voice. Plus, everything fits and the other guy mentioned him by name."

"Okay, supposing it *is* this guy, why did he have Paul killed?"

"Paul worked for Venny's Shipping, and he delivered a package to this guy. Paul saw what was in it, and this guy was afraid he'd go to the cops, so he had him killed."

"Do you know what was in the package?"

"Sure do. It was money from a drug deal in Roanoke. His partner said the buyer got caught with the drugs, but he got away with the money and mailed it to this guy here in Judsonville. Now he's hiding out in Roanoke till he can safely make it to Nashville."

"What's your mom's boyfriend's name?"

"Francis Whitman. He told her to call him Frank, and his partner called him Frankie."

"What was his partner's name?" Sam asked in an odd tone of voice.

"I don't know, but Francis called him Scotty."

Sam Buckson whistled. "I don't believe this! Scott Owens and Frank Russell? Tell me, does this Francis guy talk with a really horrid British accent and look like a cross between Tom Cruise and Harrison Ford?"

Well, I never really thought of it that way, but come to think of it . . . after all, he was definitely good looking. And there was no mistaking that absurd accent. "Yeah, that's him. And guess what?"

"What?" he asked, eagerly.

"His address is 286-A Horizon Drive. Sound familiar?"

"286AHD!"

"Yup. Now do you believe me?"

"Yes."

"Look, we need you to come—" I was interrupted by a knock on the front door.

Mom moved to the door, motioning for Luke to get down. He moved behind the counter and crouched down beside my legs as she pulled the door open. My breath caught in my throat—it was Francis. He hadn't even changed out of his nice shoes. The only difference was that he was wearing a jacket this time.

"Hi. I thought I saw someone sneak around behind your house. I tried to call you, but the line was busy, so I just wanted to make sure that everything was okay."

"Yeah," Mom replied. "Everything's fine. Must have just been the shadows or something."

I turned my back to the door. "Look," I whispered. "Now would be a great time for you to come get him."

"Is something wrong?" came the voice on the other end of the line.

"He's here," I whispered. "If he's not at home he'll probably be at my house, 285 Horizon Drive."

"Okay," Sam replied. "Hold on. We're coming."

"Hurry," I said, "and don't put on your sirens."

"Okay."

"Yeah, all right," I said in a louder voice. "Bye, Rachael." I hung up the phone and turned around to see Francis Whitman staring at me. "That was Rachael, Mom," I announced. "She just wanted to be sure I got home okay."

"No, Amy," Francis continued, picking up where he'd left off. "He was parked in the Caseys' driveway. He got out of the truck and walked around the back corner of the house. I haven't seen him come back. Something's going on. Why don't you let me check it out?"

"No really, Frank, it's okay," Mom insisted.

"Aren't you worried that some creep's wandering around out-side? Be sensible, Amy. Let me check it out. I don't want any-thing to happen to you." My blood ran cold hearing those words come from his mouth. "I'm not leaving until I check it out for you, Amy."

"All right, Frank," Mom surrendered. "Let's check it out." She stepped outside.

I glanced down. Luke gave me the "what do I do?" look. I looked back up to make sure Mom and Francis were gone and found Francis staring at me. I stood there and stared back, try-ing not to fidget, and wondering how guilty it was going to seem when I looked away. I certainly didn't want to stare at him all night.

"Do y'all see anyone out there?" I asked, desperately trying to figure out what I should do.

Francis didn't answer, but stared back at me a few moments. Without warning, he walked right past my mom and into the house.

"Frank, where are you going?" Mom called in one last des-perate attempt to call him back. I nudged Luke with my foot by way of warning, but there was nowhere for him to go. I held my gaze with Francis as he rounded the edge of the counter to face me. Then his eyes broke away from mine and moved down to settle on Luke.

I expected something like "What's going on?" or "What's he doing here?" or "Why did you lie to me, Amy?" or something like that, but Francis seemed to have taken the whole situation in with a glance.

Instead, he calmly said, "Hello, Luke Benson."

Luke didn't answer.

"I see that you and Tricia are still seeing each other out of school despite Amy's protests. I suppose I needn't ask why you were hiding from me?"

He looked back at Mom, who stood outside, still as a statue. "Come on in, Amy," he invited. When she didn't move, he added, "Really, there's no sense in freezing outside. I told you that I didn't want anything to happen to you. You still believe me, don't you?"

Mom didn't answer, but she did come inside.

"So who was that on the phone, Tricia?" he asked me. "Just curious."

"My friend Rachael."

"Who was on the phone, Tricia? It's not becoming for a young lady such as yourself to lie." I could feel my anger burning through my body, and I was powerless to stop it. The flame had leaked into my eyes before I could control it. "I see it, Tricia. You can't hide your feelings forever. Although I must admit I don't know how you found me. So, how long till they get here? Five minutes, one minute?"

I shrugged.

"Then I suppose we should be leaving, don't you?"

"What?" I snapped.

Francis leaped forward, grabbed me by the neck, and pressed something cold under my chin. "I said," he repeated slowly, "I think it's time we leave, don't you?" He turned around to face Luke. I followed suit, having very little choice in the matter since he still had a pretty tight grip on my neck and I didn't really want to choke at the moment. From the look on Luke's face, I could pretty much guess that the cold metal against my face belonged to a gun.

"Come along, Mr. Benson. You're coming too."

Luke stood without protest. Even if he didn't believe that Francis would shoot me right here and now, I knew that he wouldn't leave me alone with this creep.

"You're staying, Amy," Francis announced.

"Why?" she asked, probably the only word she could think of. I couldn't even imagine how many meanings were behind that simple question.

"To give good old Sam Buckson and his cops some extra incentive to give me some space. I'm sure he knows how upset you would be if he went and got your daughter killed. I'm sorry that things had to work out this way, Amy. I knew that I couldn't stay here forever, but I had hoped that we could be happy while

I was here—that you could help me forget Scott and the rest of it for a while. But in the end, I am who I am, and now that's what I have to be."

"Scum," she growled.

"I'm sorry, Amy." With that, he rapped her over the head with the side of his revolver and replaced it to my throat before I could even blink, much less so much as think of moving. Besides, his hand had never left my throat.

I stared in horror as Mom crumpled to the floor. "What have you done?" I screamed at him.

"She'll be all right," Francis promised. "Let's go." He dragged me out the door, leaving Luke no choice but to follow. Francis dragged me across the road to his house where he simply stepped inside and grabbed a black bag. Then he slammed the door and proceeded to drag me back across the road to Luke's truck, parked in the Caseys' drive.

"You're driving," he informed Luke. He put me in the middle and sat on the edge, being sure his gun never left my throat throughout the entire process. "All right," Francis said. "You're going to be my chauffeur. Try anything funny or don't follow my directions, and I kill her. If that happens, chances are you'll be next." Francis smiled. "Well, glad we got that out of the way. Let's go." Luke turned on the truck and backed out onto Horizon Drive. "And step on the gas a bit, would you?"

Luke cursed under his breath as he pushed down on the accelerator. For once I couldn't lecture him for cursing—whether or not I meant it I didn't know, but I was thinking the exact same thing.

CHAPTER EIGHTEEN

It wasn't long before we were on the highway headed north, leaving Judsonville far behind. I really had no clue where Francis thought he was going. If I were him, the first thing I would have done was cross the state line—Tennessee was only about forty-five minutes from Judsonville, but we were headed in the opposite direction. One thing was for sure—Francis Whitman definitely wasn't stupid. I knew better than that. He had something up his sleeve—I just hadn't figured out what yet.

I was sure about one thing, though—the gun under my chin was starting to get really uncomfortable. I glanced over at Francis, but he seemed pretty oblivious to my discomfort. Like he'd care anyway. A question was eating away at me, and the only thing stopping me from asking it was the simple fact that I wasn't sure how he would react. I remembered the old quote: "Never ask a question unless you already know the answer." It always seemed like a contradiction to me, but now I thought I knew where whoever said it was coming from. I waited until I couldn't stand it anymore, and then I looked over at Francis and said, "What was going on between you and Mom?"

"What?" he asked, moving his gaze in my direction.

"Was that just some cover-up? Did you care about her at all?"

"Of course I cared about her," Francis sighed. "I was planning on having a bit of a vacation in Judsonville and forgetting about work for a while. Unfortunately things didn't work out that way."

"Obviously," I muttered. "But you're using me," I objected. "You're using me to hurt her."

"Not exactly."

"Then what would you call it?"

"Business," Francis replied unemotionally. "Look Tricia. I like you all right, and I really don't want to hurt you. But the truth is, survival comes first, and if I have to kill you to get away, don't think I won't. I consider it your own fault for getting involved in something that was none of your business, the same as if you jumped in front of a train or tried to play fireman without the proper equipment and got burned to death."

"They're not the same, Francis," I said, horrified at his inhuman perspective.

"When you're in *my* business, they are, Tricia."

"Whatever."

"So *you* answer *me* something now," Francis suggested. "How about you tell me how you discovered me. I didn't leave any trail that could link me to Bobby Joe Fink, and I killed him before he could say anything to the police or to you."

"Purely by accident. Do you remember when you ran out of gas one day and a girl named Rachael got gas and took your trash for you?"

"Yes, vaguely."

"And I don't suppose you remember what you had in the trash along with the boxes? It seems the bag broke when she got out of the car, and this little piece of incriminating evidence fell out."

"I have no idea what you're talking about."

"Let me give you a hint. Rachael records all of the important lectures from our history teacher, Mr. Burton, and she's always running out of those little mini tapes. She picks them up wherever she finds them."

"You have the answering machine tape?" he demanded.

I shrugged. "Maybe. Tough luck, huh, Frankie?"

"Not necessarily. Not if I get away."

"Just out of curiosity," Luke said, "where are we going?"

"Somewhere."

"No duh," Luke snapped, his patience fraying a bit. "Look, I'm driving, so don't you think it would help if I knew where we were going? I don't see that it would make a whole heck of a lot of difference, do you?" he said bluntly.

"Well, I guess not," Francis replied, seeming a bit taken aback. After all he was the one with the gun. Luke didn't seem to care much anymore. "We're going to a little private airport called Quincy's Airfield. Just a little place I know where you drop your cash and get a lift, no questions asked."

"Where are you flying to?" I asked curiously, not really expecting him to tell me.

"You're coming too, little lady," he said pointedly.

"What?" I demanded.

"Still need a bit of insurance. You and your little lover boy there are going to take a bit of a vacation with me to Roanoke. We're going to pick up my buddy Scott and head to Nashville. Then we'll get rid of you two and relocate somewhere nice— Europe, maybe."

"You've got to be kidding," I protested without much conviction. Kidding? Yeah, right—I knew better than to think that Francis even knew the meaning of the word.

"So where is this airport?" Luke asked.

"Just past Fredericksville." Luke and I shared a quick glance as Francis continued. "We'll have to go through town—it's on the other side."

A tiny flutter of hope beat in my heart. Fredericksville. It just so happened that the Carrier High football team was in Fredericksville right now, playing an away game. I glanced at my watch. It was somewhere close to 9:30. Fredericksville was two hours away from Judsonville, and we had been on the road somewhere around an hour. That would put us in Fredericksville at approximately 10:30. If we could run into the football team on their way home and be recognized, we could possibly be rescued. Long shot but a possibility.

I yawned hugely, wishing I could go to sleep. I had always hated sitting in the middle for the simple reason that there was nothing for me to lean my head on. Finally I couldn't keep my eyes open any longer, so I tapped Francis on the shoulder. "I'm going to. . . ." I pointed to Luke's shoulder.

Francis shrugged, and I rested my head against Luke's shoulder. Normally I wouldn't have bothered him while he was driving, but I was burned out, and he didn't seem to mind. The last thing I remember thinking before I drifted off was the prayer for a chance meeting with the Carrier High football team and to keep Francis Whitman's finger off the trigger while I was asleep.

I woke to the sound of the Dave Matthews Band on the radio. I opened my eyes slowly, feeling a cramping pain seep into my neck. I blinked a few times, feeling the shoulder shift under my head. Hoping I hadn't caused Luke too much discomfort, I sat up, trying to blink the fogginess out of my eyes. I felt Luke's arm move as his right hand left the wheel and reached down to squeeze mine. I turned to see his gentle smile, and I smiled back, feeling a new and welcome warmth crawl into my heart. A few months ago I wouldn't have believed it possible that I could love Luke Benson as much as I did at that moment.

He reluctantly pulled his hand away and replaced it on the wheel as the DJ's voice came on over the radio. "And once again, the Carrier High Mustangs win tonight, beating the Fredericksville Bears 28-7. However, it was a mixed victory for the Mustangs—after they walked off the field, they learned that two of their classmates, Tricia Lakely and Luke Benson, had allegedly been abducted by a man believed to be involved in the Paul Sanders murder. Along the same lines, police have reported that the abducted students and their kidnapper, Francis Whitman of Judsonville, Virginia, are believed to be traveling in a gray Chevrolet with Virginia tags YNC-3677. Anyone with any information should contact Investigator Sam Buckson at 555-4689."

As the next song came on I spotted two yellow school buses traveling in the opposite direction. I caught sight of the unmistakable blue uniforms hanging from the windows as they passed us—it was the Carrier High School Marching Band, on their way home. I sighed as the buses continued on their course without slowing down.

"Speed it up a bit, would you?" Francis asked in a tone that was more suited for an order.

Luke obediently stepped on the gas, but I followed his hopeful gaze to the Fredericksville city limit sign that slid past on the side of the road. I glanced down at my watch again. Twenty-five past ten. We'd be cutting it close. My thumping heart made me feel like holding my breath, but I knew that was a premature move, unless I was planning on passing out.

I caught sight of a glowing McDonald's sign on the upcoming curve. As Luke rounded that curve, a whole stretch of restaurants, gas stations, and businesses opened up before us. And so, with high hopes and nervous, thumping hearts, we plunged right into the thick of Fredericksville.

There seemed to be about a million and a half traffic lights on this road. And I would have guessed that fully half of them were turning red just for us. I could tell that Francis was getting tense by the nervous tapping of his gun against my back. From the point of view of the casual outside observer, it would appear that he had his arm around me, but in reality, he was jabbing his gun up into my spine. Even though it was starting to be really uncomfortable, one look at Francis's rapidly darkening face and I knew better than to say a single word.

Fredericksville was a pretty decent sized place. By the time we had crawled our way through the mass of traffic lights and fast food joints, my watch read 10:35. I scanned the other lane of traffic for a pair of big gray charter buses, but I couldn't see them anywhere. As we rounded another curve and left the business district behind, I saw the huge stadium lights situated on a hill ahead to the right. And just below that hill was the complex of Fredericksville High School.

My breath caught in my throat as I caught sight of two unmistakable gray charter buses making their way down the little road toward the high school sign and the traffic light at the bottom of the hill. It was the football team leaving. As we made our way closer to the light, the first bus pulled to a stop at the bottom of the hill. Our light turned yellow as we drew nearer.

Luke began to apply the brake, but Francis Whitman barked, "Run that light, boy!" The light turned red as we came closer. The unsuspecting charter bus driver pulled out to turn. I was certain that the second driver saw us coming, and had the first bus continued at present speed, we would have cleared between it and the second. But the first bus slammed on its brakes all of a sudden and stopped, right in the middle of the intersection.

Luke clenched his teeth shut as he stomped the brake in a vain effort to bring his truck from sixty miles an hour down to zero really fast. I could tell almost immediately that we weren't going to make it. Luke's foot was against the floorboard and his hands had a death grip on the steering wheel as we skidded toward the bus. I heard Luke and Francis scream together just before the truck slammed against the side of the bus, and Francis's gun bounced out of his hand, clattering to the floorboard.

I faintly heard my own voice with theirs as the hood crumpled up, and I screamed, "Move it, Luke!" He practically kicked open his door and scrambled out, with me inches behind. I could hear Francis swearing behind me as we ran for our lives toward the front of the bus. Luke made it around the front of the bus before me, and I could hear him pounding on the doors. He scrambled aboard as I rounded the front corner, but I didn't make it.

Francis gave me a sharp shove from behind that sent me flying to the asphalt. I came up spitting blood and feeling like every bone in my body had just shattered. I turned around to see the end of Francis's pistol pointing right between my eyes.

"Move and I swear I'll kill you right here and now," Francis growled as I stared up into his eyes, my muscles locking with his words. "That's better," he said. He reached down, grabbed my wrist, and hauled me to my feet. Then he dropped my wrist and locked that arm around my waist, jabbing his gun against my head. "All right, Tricia," he said. "Be a good girl and hand over the tape."

"What?" I demanded, frantically trying to buy time.

"The tape," he repeated, digging his gun into my skin even harder. "If I get caught, I don't want to be convicted of murder, either for Paul Sanders or Bobby Joe Fink. Drug dealing I can handle, but not murder. Give me the tape."

He and I both knew that besides the word of a couple of kids the tape was the only evidence that could convict him. "No," I replied, blood still trickling out of the corner of my mouth.

"You produce that tape or they'll really have a reason to convict me of murder!" Francis threatened.

"No," I gasped.

"I'm going to count to three and then your brains get splattered across the pavement. You've seen me kill, Tricia. Don't think I won't do it to you. One," he began ominously.

God, please, I prayed desperately. "Wait! I—"

"She doesn't have it!" Luke shouted, jumping off of the charter bus.

"What?" Francis demanded.

"I do."

"Give it to me, or she dies," Francis threatened.

"All right," Luke said. "I'll give it to you."

"Show it to me," Francis ordered.

Luke looked a bit unsure for a moment as I carefully reached into my pocket and pulled out the mini tape. He didn't have it—I did. I tossed it to him, and he caught it and held it up. "Here it is," he said.

"You lied to me!" Francis screamed at Luke, then he twisted the gun against my skull.

"But I have it now, and I'll give it to you if you let her go," he promised, taking a step forward. "Take it and run. Nobody here can stop you. What do you say?"

There was a long pause during which nobody moved except Aaron and Joe, who clambered off the charter bus to stare at the three of us, followed momentarily by Coach Jones, who stood behind them. "Deal," Francis said finally.

Luke walked forward, holding out the tape. As Francis let go of me to reach for the tape, I ducked out of his grasp, snatched the tape from Luke's fingers, and threw it back at Aaron and Joe. Luke grabbed Francis's gun with both hands, trying to wrestle it free from his grasp. I hesitated only a moment before yanking my foot back and launching the most powerful kick I could muster. The blow was right on target, nailing Francis in a *very* tender spot. The gun slid from his fingers as he fell rearward.

The force of my kick sent me stumbling backwards, and I fell into Aaron's ready arms as Francis Whitman slammed against the pavement. Luke pointed the gun down at Francis as I regained my feet. Aaron stood beside me as Joe walked forward to join us, the mini tape clutched in his hand.

"Don't move," Luke growled.

Francis laughed weakly. "You wouldn't shoot me."

"Maybe he wouldn't, but I sure would." Coach Jones reached out his hand and Luke handed him the gun. "And there's a bunch of guys on those two buses who are real fired up from just winning a game. I think I could talk a couple of the linemen into decking you if you moved."

"I don't see any of them out here," Francis pointed out.

"Move," Aaron said in a deep, menacing voice. "I dare you, slimeball. I'm no guppy myself, you know."

Francis groaned as an unmarked Buick pulled across from the opposite lane, a blue light flashing from its dash. The driver's door opened, and Sam Buckson stepped out. The other three doors opened with Tommy Hall getting out of the passenger seat and a man and woman I didn't recognize emerging from the backseat.

They seemed to know Luke, however. The woman all but screamed his name as she caught sight of him. Luke turned around and, forgetting all male dignity, ran straight to his mother's arms.

"Arrest him," Sam Buckson said to his partner, pointing to Francis, who still lay sprawled across the northbound lane of the road.

Tommy Hall nodded and marched over to the scene. Coach Jones lowered Francis's gun, and Tommy Hall roughly rolled Francis over and handcuffed his hands behind his back. "You're under arrest for murder. You have the right to remain silent. Anything you say can and will be used against you in a court of law. You have the right to an attorney. . . ."

I turned away as Sam walked up to the three of us. Joe handed me the tape, which I also gave to Sam. "There you go," I said. "Proper evidence."

"We were headed this direction and only about forty minutes away when we got a call on my cell phone from the band, who had heard the radio broadcast and said they'd seen your truck heading into Fredericksville. We got here as fast as we could."

"I'm not going to ask how fast you were driving," I laughed weakly.

"What happened here?" he asked gently. I was conscious again of the dried blood around my mouth. I probably looked horrible. "Your mother said that Francis saw Luke in your house and knew that you knew, so he hit her over the head and took you two. When she woke up, she said Luke's truck was gone and Francis's car was still there. We sent her to the hospital to be checked out. They called us back and said she only had a mild concussion."

"Francis was going to take us to an airport close to here and we were going to fly to Roanoke to pick up his partner."

"When they didn't find him anywhere in Tennessee, I figured he was going for his partner," Sam nodded.

"Yeah. Luke was driving, and Francis told him to run this light, but the bus pulled out and stopped, and we wrecked. Francis dropped his gun in the crash, so we made a run for it. Luke made it to the bus, but Francis pushed me down and told me if I didn't give him the phone tape he'd kill me. Then I threw it to Luke, and Luke said he'd trade Francis the tape for me. During the handoff, I got away, threw the tape back to Aaron and Joe, and Luke wrestled the gun away from him."

"Just out of curiosity, how'd he end up on the ground?" Sam asked.

I blushed. "I kicked him."

"Oh," Sam replied, a smile tugging at the corners of his mouth. "Need I ask where?"

"No," I replied quickly.

Coach Jones joined us, plopping Francis's gun into Sam's hand. "What happened with the bus?" Sam asked.

"We were pulling out," Coach Jones said, "and Aaron and

Joe started yelling 'there they are!' or something to that effect, so I told the driver to block the intersection. Then the truck plowed into our side. The bus jerked a bit, but that's all. I don't think they were going real fast when they hit us. Just fast enough to not stop in time, you know."

Sam nodded as Luke finally walked up beside me, making our company complete. "There's an ambulance coming, and I'm going to have you two checked out," Sam said, gesturing to Luke and me. Just then, we heard a siren. "That should be him," he added.

The ambulance pulled up, and Sam led us over to it. I looked back over my shoulder as Tommy ducked Francis's head into the car and shut the door behind him. Francis stared at me, giving me the most evil look I'd ever seen in my life.

"See you in court, you loser!" I shouted at him. Since Mom wasn't here, I figured I would have to take the honors. Then I turned my back on him and walked away, never to look back.

I looked up at the twinkling stars again and winked. *For you, Paul,* I thought. *I did this for you.* As the back doors of the ambulance opened, I turned to Aaron and Joe, standing behind us. We stood there looking at each other and I thrust out my hand, palm down. Aaron grinned and placed his hand on top of mine, followed by Joe and Luke. We never spoke—we just stood there in our circle for a long moment before finally drawing our hands back.

The paramedics helped Luke and me into the ambulance. Aaron, Joe, Sam, Coach Jones, and Luke's parents stood outside while we were looked over. It took the paramedics a while to clean up the scrapes all over my arms and the cut just above my mouth. Then they told the waiting group that they were going to take us to the hospital and run a couple of X rays and such to make sure that there was no internal damage—lah-de-dah. I wasn't really listening. My eyes were buried in Luke's gaze.

I turned to give Aaron and Joe one final wink before the doors closed between us. My gaze returned to Luke's face as the ambulance began to move. Everything in the ambulance faded away, until there were only the two of us left. Luke leaned forward and kissed me as my arms slid around his neck and my eyes slowly closed. The pain of my scrapes and aching body eased away until all I could sense was him. I held him close, hoping that this moment would last a long, long time.

EPILOGUE

The snow flurries caught on my eyelashes as I blinked. I wasn't sure if I would ever be warm again, but at the moment I really didn't care. Most sane people wouldn't willingly venture outside in weather like this—a snowy day with a temperature at twenty below with windchill. Of course the word *sane* wouldn't necessarily have applied to the crowd of screaming people around me. I can say for a fact that I wasn't completely rational at the moment. I was, however, experiencing one of the most wonderful, exhilarating, breathtaking, memorable moments of my teenage life.

I was at a football game. And it wasn't just any football game. The crowd gathered at Walter Camp Field hadn't come because they didn't have anything better to do on a freezing Saturday afternoon. They hadn't come to see a major rivalry played out— these two teams had never before met on the football field. They hadn't even come merely to see if Judsonville could add one more win to their record. They were here for something even greater—to see a state championship won.

It was late in the fourth quarter, and the game was tied. The blood red King High Cobras were driving mercilessly toward the goal line and the win. The men on the field and the crowd in the stands were determined not to let them have it, however. We screamed and screamed, as if our voices feared they would never be heard again.

I relentlessly fought the numbness that seeped in through my red ears and nose as our boys lined up bravely on the line of scrimmage, knowing what they wanted and ready to take it. I could barely feel my toes as I jumped up and down, but I could feel the warm hand that Luke held just fine. I turned and grinned at him, waiting to see what was going to happen.

The ball was snapped and the twenty-two forms on the field surged into motion. Players scattered, and the Cobra quarterback yanked his arm back and launched the ball high into the air for a long pass. He was going for it all. I held my breath as Luke's hand squeezed in time to his whispered chant of, "Don't catch it, don't catch it. . . ." Two figures outshot the rest, one a red Cobra, one a blue Mustang. The ball was coming closer— either one of them could catch it.

"Please!" I whispered as the Mustang turned to receive the ball, and the white number on his jersey reflected in the sun. It was very probable that the outcome of the AA Division 3 Virginia State Championship game rested on the shoulders of number 22.

Luke's fingers cut off the blood flow to my hand as they squeezed harder than ever, his chant changing to "Catch it, catch it. . . ."

And then the ball fell from the sky, right through the leaping grasp of the red Cobra and directly into the ready hands of Joe Taylor. A scream arose from the student section and echoed across the stadium to the home side as the Cobra slid to the dirt and what was left of the yellowing grass, and Joe Taylor tore back down the field.

A new cheer emerged from the mass of screaming teenagers that took form in the words "Go Joe! Go Joe!" Our voices roared down the field, no doubt carrying all the way to number 22 and giving him the power to break five tackles and sprint to the fifteen yard line before finally being slung to the ground by the dumbfounded Cobra offense.

Joe dropped the ball and sprang to his feet, only to be nearly tackled again by his teammates. Their shouts carried to the stands as the victorious defense trotted off the field to be replaced by a newly energized and pumped up offense. One thing was for sure—players and fans alike were ready to seal this game in favor of our own Carrier High Mustangs.

The snow swirled down around our heads as the players lined up, but for some reason, it didn't seem real. Everything on and around Walter Camp Field seemed to fade away like a memory from a dream. In fact, as my world narrowed, only two things remained as a solid reminder of reality: the center's hand on the football and the warm hand that held my own. The world came crashing back with breathtaking force as the ball surged into Steve Johnson's steady hands.

The pitch to Jared Hutchins was so subtle that I almost missed it, but there was no mistaking the brown football tucked in number 3's right arm as he took off across the line of scrimmage like there was a real cobra after him. Actually, he might have preferred a snake to the big, pounding, and overly ticked-off-looking defensive guys hot on his tail.

Two of the guys closed from each side, their huge arms surrounding Jared in an effort to slam him to the turf. And then it happened—the football popped right out of Jared's hands and bounced against the frozen ground.

Two hands closed on the football and clasped it to their owner's chest. The football player, who would never have ordinarily carried the ball, slid right through two attackers and sprinted for all he was worth as if he had run this same play a hundred times before. As number 99 plowed through two defenders and plunged across the goal line, the entire student section surged to its feet as one, shouting for the whole world and even the stars to hear. Before I knew it, every single teenager in the vicinity—including me—was bouncing up and down on toes that felt like coiled springs. "Yeah Aaron!" I shrieked at the top of my lungs, somehow screaming, laughing, and crying at the same time as the clock dwindled down to zero.

The crowd was pouring onto the field almost before the extra point kick had split the uprights, making the final score 21-14. Both teams shook hands, and then all eyes turned to behold the sunbeam reflecting from the surface of the golden football mounted on the state championship trophy. I don't remember the announcer's words as the trophy was presented; I just remember the mindless and absolutely beautiful screams of my friends and schoolmates.

I do remember with absolute clarity, however, the identical looks on the faces of Aaron Tyler and Joe Taylor when Luke and I finally found them in the crowd. That sparkling in their eyes and amazed, joyful expression would live in my memory forever. This time it was Aaron's hand that surged into the middle of our circle first, Joe's hand covering it almost instantaneously. Luke grinned and added his to the stack, and I laughed, placing mine on top. And then the four of us, basking in the presence of trusted friends, burst out laughing all at once. I could never put the precise reason for our laughter into words, but I can truthfully say that it was something so wonderful that words would probably only have spoiled the moment—that sort of thing could only be expressed with a smile and pure and simple laughter. And so we laughed.

The Mustang team around us began to sink to their knees, preparing for the coach's closing prayer after the game. The four of us knelt as well and reached for the hand of the person next to us.

I don't remember the coach's prayer, but I do remember the feel of Aaron's and Joe's hands in mine and Luke's smile as I thought, *Thank you God, for everything. And give my love to Paul.*